The Last Snow Dragon

Diana Winter

ASPIRE
PUBLISHING HUB LLC.

The Last Snow Dragon
Copyright © 2022 by Diana Winter

ISBN
978-1-958692-62-2 (Paperback)
978-1-958692-63-9 (eBook)

Dedication

This book is dedicated to my darling little "Toads," young and older. For without them, it would not exist, and especially to Mom.

Prelude

In very ancient times before the ice ages, before the great flood, before the knights of King Arthur, and even before Rome's great empire was the first time of man. It is a time now forgotten by history. Little knowledge of it remains to even speak of except mythological tales. In that forgotten age, magical creatures and great beasts lived together. It is in this time this tale unfolds in a valley rich in ancient lore. It was in the Valley of the Dragon.

The Valley of the Dragon was once a fertile, beautiful place with green fields, winding rivers, and streams that fed the farms and their crops. Little villages and farm houses dotted the land of the valley. No one really remembered why it was called the Valley of the Dragon, but rumored tales told of it once being the breeding grounds of the great dragons before the faerie folk tamed them and took them into their fold. One great dragon remained though. The dragon belonged to the black faerie Dorcha Oidhche who was the Faerie of the Dark Night, the faerie of nightmares. Dorcha and her dragon lived at the head of the valley on the Mountain of the Dark Shadow. Her tower sat on the tall dark cliffs surrounded by a shroud of dark mist. Dorcha affectionately called her great black dragon her *Dóitẻẚin Dubh Droch*, which meant in the old language, "bad black fire." The people of the valley just called him Droch. For he was bad any way they saw him. Droch had a terrible reputation, as terrible as a ferocious dog that was left untamed by his careless master.

For centuries Dorcha and her dragon did not bother the people of the valley. The snow faerie Geal Geamhradh, also known as the winter queen, had forbid her of doing any harm to the valley and its people. Geal was the faerie ruler of the land. Dorcha was only allowed to visit nightmares on the wicked and wrong doers to punish them for their transgressions. Dorcha was a very angry and evil dark faerie who liked to play mean tricks and cause dissention between people and faeries alike. None of the other faeries liked her, and over the centuries, little by little, they left Dorcha out of their games and celebrations. Dorcha always spoiled their fun. Because of her evil ways, she was shunned from the company of the other faeries, which made Dorcha even more angry and rebellious. Then one day after she was shunned again from the summer solstice celebration, Dorcha became very angry and decided to let Droch loose in the Valley of the Dragon. If she were to be outcast from her kind, then she would outcast them as well, including the winter queen and her rules. There was little the winter queen could do to her; after all, Faeries were almost immortal, and it was forbidden to kill one of their own. Once born from whatever element, plant, or natural force of nature they came from, a Faerie lived an eternal life. They never withered or aged like other creatures. However, a Faerie could be destroyed by force. No matter what punishment Geal handed down, Dorcha decided to disregard it. She was through with the other faeries and would do as she pleased.

Dorcha started out slowly, letting Droch fly through the valley at night to eat cattle and naughty children who didn't come in from play after dark. She often stood on the balcony of her tower and laughed as she watched him swoop down the Mountain of the Dark Shadow to the valley below. She had all summer and most of fall to ruin the valley before winter came. The winter queen didn't venture out until the first snow. Other faeries had abandoned the valley to get away from Dorcha and her cruel games. None of the faerie folk would know what she had done until it was too late.

After a while, the cattle became scarce, parents didn't let their children out to play after dark anymore, and the dragon turned to eating anyone or anything. When the black dragon could no longer find enough cattle and people, the dragon turned to hunting in the daylight hours, destroying homes and other buildings in the valley. With most the cattle eaten and people too afraid to go out and tend the fields for fear of being eaten by Droch, the valley became a place of poverty, devastation, and fear. By winter the Valley had been completely destroyed. On the eve of the winter solstice, the snow faerie Geal Geamhradh, the winter queen, was out enjoying a ride on her old white snow dragon when she came across the Valley of the Dragon. Though Geal was thought to be cold and uncaring, it was on that day the people discovered she was instead a warm hearted soul. Upon seeing the starving cold people and devastation of the valley, she turned herself into a poor beggar woman and went to the main village of the Valley of the Dragon to find out why the valley was in such despair.

Geal entered the village and saw starvation and death. She asked the people why they were so bad off. They explained about Dorcha and what her dragon had done. Dorcha had let her dragon destroy the valley. Though they didn't have much to spare, the people shared what they had with Geal anyway and offered her a warm place to stay. They felt sorry for the old beggar woman as they themselves knew what it was like to go hungry and lose their homes. Geal was touched by their kindness and stayed the night with the people. But in the morning she had vanished. No one knew where she had gone. They thought perhaps she had strayed out in the night and the dragon had eaten her.

Geal had indeed strayed out in the night, and, yes, the dragon had found her, but by then she had turned back into the snow faerie. A battle erupted between the snow queen's great white snow dragon known as Bain the White Dragon and the great black dragon Droch. Dorcha's dragon had descended upon them in an attack, but Geal's white dragon loved her mistress and vowed no harm would come to her. Even though the white dragon was old, she won the fight; however, she was badly wounded. In her anger and anguish over the wounds of her white dragon and the harm Droch had caused, Geal turned Droch into a frozen rock never again to plague the people of the Valley of the Dragon. Geal then went to the dark faerie Dorcha and told her she would do the same to her if she ever again let a dragon destroy the valley or did any harm to its people and their lives. But Dorcha just laughed at her. Dorcha knew Geal could not harm her according to the faerie law. And then who would send the nightmares to punish the wicked? Geal was more cleaver than Dorcha though and told her laws could be changed and that there were many ways to punish the wicked besides nightmares. Dorcha was very angry at the snow faerie, but Geal, who was a faerie queen after all, was far more powerful than Dorcha, and Dorcha knew Geal could call the counsel of faeries to change the law. Reluctantly Dorcha agreed she would do as Geal ordered. She would not harm the valley anymore, but there were other things she could harm. Inside Dorcha was seething with anger and malice towards the Winter Queen. Dorcha would wait until something would avail itself, and then secretly she would plan her vengeance on the winter queen.

Geal returned to the village, but this time as the winter queen of the faeries, and thanked the people for their kindness. Geal told them what she had done to Dorcha's dragon and that Dorcha would never again destroy the valley or the people's lives. The people of the Valley of the Dragon thanked the winter queen and held a great celebration in her honor. Every year on the winter solstice, a great celebration was held for the winter queen. It became a holy day of thanks and giving to everyone, especially those less fortunate, and a celebration of life even in the dead of winter.

Chapter 1

It had been several years since the white dragon, Bain, had battled with the black dragon, Droch. Geal watched helplessly as her old friend finally succumbed to her wounds that would never quite heal. There was no magic or medicine that could work against the dark poison of the black dragon for long. Geal had tried many things over and over to save the great white dragon. Bain had fought to live on out of love for her mistress and didn't want to leave her, but now the great white dragon could no longer fight against the illness. She had become too old and weak to overcome her wounds from her battle with the black dragon, and after a few years of struggling, finally died. Geal was saddened by the death of her old friend. Bain had been a very good companion to the winter queen, and Bain was the last great snow dragon. Not wanting Geal to be left alone, the white dragon left one last gift for Geal. It was an egg. From the egg hatched another great white snow dragon, the child of Geal's old friend Bain, the great white Dragon. Geal was overcome with joy. She loved the baby white dragon and named him *Sneachta Dhragain*, Snow Dragon.

One day in early winter, Geal stood on a balcony of her ice palace with her dragon hatchling in her arms. She affectionately stroked his back as she looked down across the valley. There she saw a pristine winter wonderland. The virgin snow that covered everything sparkled in the sun light. She gazed toward the loch and saw pine and fir trees heavily laden with snow on their branches. Geal marveled at how peaceful and serene her realm looked. She decided it was a splendid day to take Sneachta down from her ice castle and past the mystic loch into the forest below to play in the first snow of winter. While there, Geal saw a group of snow bunnies playing games and happily chatting with each other. An older snow bunny by the name of Snozzel approached Geal as she sat with Sneachta watching them. Snozzel and Geal were great friends. Sneachta jumped from Geal's arms and ran to play with the other snow bunnies.

Snozzel then bowed low before the Winter Queen and said, "Your Grace I have put aside a bit of dandelion tea for winter store. Would you care to join me in a cup?"

"I would be honored Snozzel. It would be a perfect cap for such a delightful day," Geal replied. Geal rarely had visitors because she was an ice faerie, and no one wanted to freeze for long in her cold realm during visits. Most faeries never came out in the cold season as it was. No faerie would venture into Geal's cold realm unless it was on important business. She longed for company and was overcome with joy at the snow bunny's invitation. After accepting Snozzel's invitation, he hopped away and in a few moments returned with a hot tea pot of dandelion tea, napkins, and cups. Geal was so caught up in laughing and telling tales with the snow bunny she didn't notice that Sneachta had wandered out of her sight away from the other snow bunnies. He was still quite a small dragon, and he had not yet shed his baby skin and could not yet fly. Geal had not had a baby dragon in so long that she had forgotten how curious and troublesome little dragons could be. They were always scampering off exploring and getting into things they shouldn't. Soon Sneachta was far away from his mistress and lost in the snow covered woods.

As Sneachta had wandered deep into the woods, he had been watched by an unusually large black raven. The raven quietly followed Sneachta. After some time Sneachta realized he was lost. He could not find his way back to Geal. Sneachta tried to retrace his tracks in the snow, but they went around in circles and crisscrossed each other to the point he could not tell which direction he came from. Finally Sneachta came to an old oak tree and whimpered to himself. Up above on the branches, the raven watched him and then asked, "Why are you crying little one?"

Startled, Sneachta looked up, cringing against the trunk of the oak tree.

"Don't be afraid. I won't hurt you," the raven gently cawed to put the baby dragon at ease.

"I'm lost," Sneachta finally replied.

"I can help you," said the raven.

Sneachta looked up at the raven suddenly feeling hopeful again. "You can?" he asked.

"Aye, I can carry you back home if you like," the raven offered. Being so young and naïve, the baby dragon accepted the raven's help.

The raven swooped down from its perch and took Sneachta in its talons. As the raven flew up again into the sky, Sneachta was overcome with excitement. He had never flown before. He wished he could spread his little wings and flutter them in the air, but the raven had them pinned down under its grasp. "Do you know where I live?" asked Sneachta.

The raven looked down at him. "No, but maybe you can tell me," replied the raven.

"I live on the ice mountain," Sneachta said.

"Then I will look for an ice mountain," said the raven, "But perhaps you might like to fly a little while with me. I have no friends, you see, and it would be a very nice day for me if we could play a while before I take you home," the raven added.

Sneachta was so captivated by the sensation of being airborne and by the view below him that he quickly agreed. "But just for a little while. My aunt will worry if I don't come back soon," Sneachta said.

After a long time had passed, Sneachta finally realized the raven was taking him farther from home. He panicked when he realized he was too far away from his beloved Aunt Geal.

"Please, can you take me back now?" Sneachta begged. But the raven did not answer. "I want to go home now. Can we go back?" Sneachta asked again. The raven's only reply to his request was an evil snicker. Sneachta then knew something was wrong. He became frightened and anxious. Sneachta struggled in the grasp of the talons, but they were too strong. He was tightly pinned in the claws that circled his tiny body. Hours and hours passed, and by the time the raven was flying across the Valley of the Dragon, Sneachta's anxiety had turned to anger. The raven had turned a deaf ear to Sneachta's begging. Sneachta thought of a way to get the raven's attention. He screeched and wailed and called out strange, high-pitched sounds, but the raven flew on and on. Finally, as a last desperate attempt to get the raven's attention, Sneachta turned his head up and bit the raven's leg very, very hard and deep. Crying out in pain, the raven dropped the baby dragon.

Sneachta was too young to fly yet. He flapped his tiny little wings to no avail as the ground came up swift and fast below him. Sneachta felt his little dragon heart break as he thought of Geal and how she would never know what happened to him. "I'm sorry, Aunt Geal!" Sneachta cried out as he plummeted to the ground. If only he had never wandered off! Sneachta blamed himself for his entire predicament. As Sneachta hit the ground in a puff of snow, the raven cried out a loud and evil laughter. The raven touched down on the ground beside Sneachta. While it looked down upon the still body of the little dragon it's wings turned into arms of flesh and its feathers a flowing shroud of black robe. The raven's head turned to that of a woman with long, silky black hair. The raven had transformed into Dorcha. Dorcha laughed as she watched the still body of the baby dragon lying in the snow.

After poking the limp body of the baby dragon to see if it still lived, Dorcha said with a sneer, "Serves you right, you frosty cold-blooded queen!" Dorcha finally had her revenge. She had destroyed Geal's dragon as Geal had destroyed hers. The winter queen would never know it was she who took her baby snow dragon. If Geal looked into her magic chalice of truth, she would only see a raven. Laughing in evil glee, Dorcha transformed again into a raven and flew home to her tower on the Mountain of the Dark Shadow.

Back at the forest below the ice mountain, Geal searched and searched but could not find Sneachta. Unbeknownst to Geal, Sneachta was far away. She did not know he had fallen in the Valley of the Dragon.

After some time Geal gave up on searching for Sneachta in the woods and hurried back to her ice palace. There she melted the ice in her magic chalice of truth to see if it could reveal where her little dragon was. The reflection in the icy water of the chalice brought forth confusing scenes of Sneachta's disappearance. that left Geal very puzzled and frightened. Frustrated, Geal paced back and forth trying to make sense out of what she had just seen in her magic chalice of truth. The grief she suffered was almost unbearable when she thought of Sneachta being lost out in the wild. Geal was very angry at herself for not paying more attention to her precious baby dragon, to her charge entrusted to her by the great white dragon, her sacred friend's last gift. Geal felt she had betrayed Bain somehow by being neglectful. She had forgotten how curious and troublesome baby dragons could be. Geal had let Sneachta slip away. Through the magic chalice, Geal saw through Sneachta's eyes. She saw the snow covered forest and the flapping of large black wings and the talons that encircled Sneachta as he traveled through the air and then nothing. Absolutely nothing! She didn't know if the nothing meant Sneachta was no more. Did the large black bird eat the baby dragon? But as she searched deep within her heart, she felt that Sneachta still lived. Sneachta had to still be alive; Geal would not accept anything else. If Sneachta was still out there, he would be frightened, hungry, and the target of many hungry beasts, and the storms of the cold season would not help him find his way home any. At least Sneachta was a snow dragon; he could survive the winter cold.

Geal was tempted to put winter on hold until Sneachta could be found, though she would regret doing so. For without the continued snowfall, there would not be any to melt in the spring to feed the rivers and lakes and soak the soil for new plants to sprout and grow. It would cause a devastating drought throughout the whole land. The other creatures of the land would be very angry at her and not consider the death of new life and others worth the life of just one dragon. To be a true queen meant she had to sacrifice her own needs over the needs of those in her care. A true queen had to think of the higher, greater good over her own emotional desires.

Geal had to find Sneachta quickly. Every moment that passed gave Sneachta less chance to survive. She had asked many lesser faeries, snow creatures, brownies, and the very-difficult-to-work-with pixies to help look for Sneachta. But it was hard to convince them to go out during cold season. The Dwarves of the good earth would not go out into the winter either, but at least they agreed to keep an eye out for Sneachta. Dragons were of no help; they refused to travel out into the cold unless they were hungry. Dragons liked to be kept warm. Only snow dragons would go out, and the only one left that she knew of was Sneachta. So much snow had already fallen since Sneachta disappeared. It would be almost impossible to find him. Geal wondered just how far away Sneachta had been taken. Geal also wondered what kind of black bird had taken Sneachta. It was a very large bird, and in her land there were no large black birds except ravens, vultures, and wyverns. But ravens were not as large as the bird that had taken Sneachta. It wasn't a vulture or wyvern; the talons that held Sneachta were not the same. Suddenly a thought came to Geal. Could it be an evil faerie? An evil faerie could turn into a large black bird. But which one could it be? There were several. It couldn't be Dorcha; Dorcha knew Geal would destroy her for such an act. Dorcha had promised Geal she would do no further harm.

Geal went to her private quarters and put on her winter veil. When she left her room, she walked down the great hall past the ice sculptures of the previous snow dragons she had kept in the past. As she stood at the last one, the one of her beloved Bain, she felt great sorrow. Sneachta was the last of the snow dragons. In fact, everywhere dragons were disappearing, all kinds of dragons. Geal sobbed. In her carelessness, she had let the last great snow dragon fall. She wiped her tears away and then turned and quickly left the hall. Standing on the balcony of her ice castle, Geal spread her wings and then flew to the edge of the woods where Sneachta disappeared. She had followed his trail right after he vanished, but then it stopped cold at the base of an old oak tree in the forest. She started her search once again right where it had left off. As she stood under the old oak tree, she called for a winter wind and rode it through the woods. She would not rest until Sneachta was found.

Chapter 2

Summer had gone, fall was at its end, and winter was now into its season in the Valley of the Dragon. The fall harvest, meager as it was, had been the best ever since the destruction of the valley by the great black dragon, Droch. The people were very happy. Many years had passed since the winter queen had destroyed Dorcha's dragon. The Valley of the Dragon was slowly becoming a beautiful place again. The fields that had been neglected for so long were now planted again, and cattle began to multiply as well. The valley was well on its way to prosperity and happiness once more. In the valley at its western edge was a little boy named Torin who lived with his mother, father, and two older brothers. He was a very happy child who was loved very much by his family. But little Torin's farm had been the worst hit by Droch, as it had been on the edge of the valley and was easily attacked by the dragon. Though the family had a good harvest and more cattle, they still had not enough to get through the winter very well. The destruction had been so bad they had to completely rebuild the farm and till the scorched earth over and over every season to get anything to grow again. Dragon's fire went deep into the earth, causing the soil to be less fertile. They did not want to eat their cattle and other farm animals until they had grown in numbers enough to keep it replenished. So to make up for their meager harvest, they often went hunting. It was on just such a day on the first day of snow little Torin's life would be changed forever.

Returning home from a hunting trip with his brothers and father across the rocky edge of the valley, Torin spotted a small, long, white thing lying in a snowdrift. Thinking it was an odd thing, Torin ran over to examine it. It was a strange looking large white lizard that looked as if it were dead. Being a curious little boy and doing what a little boy naturally would, Torin reached down and touched the white lizard. It was warm, and as Torin looked closer, he saw it was still breathing. "Look a lizard!" Torin exclaimed. Torin's father looked down at the lizard and shook his head. "Dad, can I keep it?" Growing cold and tired from carrying their successful hunt over his shoulders, Torin's father, whose name was Ernst was anxious to get home.

"No, your mother wouldn't like having a dead lizard in the house!" he replied.

"But it's not dead!" Torin protested.

Torin's oldest brother, Micheál, came over to examine the creature. "Yeah, but it soon will be. It looks like it has been lying here too long."

Torin's second older brother, Alsandar, came and looked down at the lizard. "Hey! Maybe we can stuff it?"

Frustrated by the delay, Torin's father yelled, "*No*! Now let's go. This is heavy, and it's getting dark!" Sadly, Torin started to walk away behind the other three, but then he decided at the last minute to turn back and grab the little white lizard and secretly stuff it away in his coat where it was warm and dry.

Once home, Torin quickly put the little lizard in a warm box lined with an old shirt. His room was behind the wall of the great kitchen hearth, and the warmth from the great hearth on the other side kept his room very warm and comfortable in the winter. Torin put the box in a hole on the hearth's back wall that was not re-bricked during repairs to the house. He used it as a secret hiding place. After his evening meal, Torin went back to his room and gave the lizard a piece of venison he had stashed in his pocket from dinner and a small broken teacup of water. The lizard had been curled up in a small ball and was snoozing comfortably. Torin watched the white lizard as it slept. He lifted his candle to get a closer look. Now that the lizard was dry and warm he noticed something odd. It had thin membranes protruding from its back, and Torin realized they were tiny little wings. He had been in too much haste before to notice much in his dark room. He had been called down to dinner and barely had time to stash the lizard. The smell of venison woke the lizard. He stretched and yawned and sniffed the meat. The lizard quickly stood up and gobbled it down as if it was half starved. "Thank you," said the small lizard.

"You talk?" Torin asked, surprised.

"Yes, I can talk," answered the lizard.

"I've never seen a talking lizard before," Torin replied.

"I'm not a lizard!" the lizard huffed as if it was insulted. "I'm a dragon."

Torin was stunned. It wasn't a lizard he had saved but a dragon! There was no way he could secretly hide a dragon for very long, let alone keep a dragon, especially after what the valley had been through in the past. His parents would be furious with him.

"Oh my, oh my!" said Torin as he walked around in circles trying to think of what to do next. He should have listened to his father and left the little dragon there. In fact, Torin was certain that as soon as his family found out he had a baby dragon, they would kill it. Suddenly another awful thought entered Torin's mind. There could be only one reason another dragon would be in the valley—a replacement for the one lost. "Are you Dorcha's new dragon?" Torin asked. The little dragon's eyes grew wide.

"Dorcha! No, I do not belong to that evil faerie!" replied the dragon. Torin was relieved.

"Then do you belong to anyone?" Torin asked.

The little dragon burped from gulping down his dinner too quickly. Giggling from embarrassment, the little dragon said, "I belong to my Aunt Geal. I got lost in the woods and was taken from her by a large raven that was probably going to eat me. But then I bit it, and it dropped me. I fell a long way."

The little white dragon then took a few gulps of water to wash down his hastily eaten meal. "Oh, I'm sorry!" Torin replied, feeling sad for the trouble the little dragon had been through.

"It's okay. I wasn't hurt too bad, but then you came along and rescued me. For that I am grateful."

"Oh aye, no problem." Torin said as he thought about the name "Geal" He had never heard of such a strange name before, and he was certain no one around here was named Geal. "Where does Geal live?" asked Torin.

"Far, far away, I'm afraid. I was flown here by the raven," said the dragon as it wept.

"Oh, I'm sorry," replied Torin. He felt sorry for the small dragon. Torin had a compassionate heart and hated to see any creature suffer for any reason. Torin softly stroked the dragons back trying to comfort him. "Do you have a name?" asked Torin.

"My name is Sneachta," replied the dragon.

Torin felt torn between fear of what his parents and the people of the valley would do when they found out he had a dragon and his sympathy for the baby dragon. Sneachta was still small, yet he probably could not survive on his own right, especially in the cold winter. There was little to eat in the winter, and wild animals would eat him. Torin didn't know Sneachta was a snow dragon. As far as Torin knew, dragons needed the warmth to survive. Torin knew the baby dragon would grow, and it would be hard to hide it then.

Sneachta curled up again and softly wept. "I miss my Aunt Geal. She is a kind lady. I want to go home. She will be worried and sad," Sneachta said through his tears. Torin thought about how he would feel if he had been taken far away from his family. Sneachta was a child just like Torin was. Torin felt empathy and compassion towards Sneachta. He wanted to help the little dragon.

"You rest now, Sneachta, and we will think of something. I promise," Torin told the dragon as he tucked a part of the old shirt around the baby dragon to help it keep warm.

Who is Geal? Torin wondered. She would have to be a faerie or some other powerful being. Common folk didn't keep dragons; it took magic to have a dragon. Dragons didn't respect anyone without powers. His second oldest brother, Alsandar, was an apprentice sorcerer, but he would not be strong enough for many years yet to control a dragon. And even then Alsandar wanted to have the dragon stuffed. Alsandar remembered the reign of terror by Dorcha's dragon, and he didn't like dragons. His oldest brother, Micheál, was good with large animals. Before Dorcha's dragon destroyed the valley, he wanted to be a dragoneer and work with a good faerie taking care of their dragons, but now he hated dragons.

Since dragons lived in the same realm as humans, the faeries often had humans who were gifted enough to help in the hatcheries and train the dragons to get along with humans and faeries alike. Suddenly a picture of his mother loomed in Torin's mind. She was standing over him shaking a large wooden spoon at him and yelling at him saying, "What were you thinking?" Torin envisioned his father taking his great sword and hacking the baby dragon to pieces in great anger. There was no one Torin could turn to for help. He would have to figure this problem out on his own. One thing was for sure: He was not going to let the baby dragon come to harm, and he would have to find away to help Sneachta return home.

The next morning Torin rose early, and before his family woke, he snuck down to the cold larder and took some more venison for Sneachta. Throughout the day Torin thought of ways to get the dragon home. He could not let Sneachta return on its own for fear the little dragon would not make it. The outer world was a dangerous place with dangerous creatures. Large saber tooth cats, wyverns, rogue dragons, and grizzly bears roamed the wild country, and they would hunt and eat Sneachta before he had a chance to get home. Then Torin had an idea he thought might work best. He would have to go out with Sneachta and find a good faerie that could help the baby dragon. He wondered where they lived and how hard it would be in the winter to find one. They generally didn't come out during the cold season, but maybe some did. Torin didn't know much about the faerie folk.

Torin wondered what kind of dragon Sneachta was. There were many kinds. Dorcha's dragon was a great dragon, the largest and most powerful of all. He had seen a great dragon before when he was just a baby, but he didn't remember it. When the winter queen came to save the valley, she had a white great dragon that didn't harm people. Sneachta was white, but that didn't mean anything. Dragons came in different sizes and colors. Sneachta was so small, so it was hard for Torin to see it as a great dragon. *Great dragons couldn't possibly be so small when they were young,* Torin thought. He wondered if Sneachta were a boy or a girl. Torin had been so surprised by his discovery that Sneachta was really a dragon that he hadn't thought to ask.

The next day Torin's father had kept him busy all morning helping his older brothers clean out the barn and feed the cows, chickens, and pigs. In the afternoon he then had to help his mom clean the house while the older brothers went hunting again with their father. Torin had little time during the day to check on Sneachta and find out more about the dragon. It wasn't until after dinner Torin finally had time to check on the little dragon. The dragon was curled up with little dragon sized tears running down its nose. "I'm sorry I left you alone for so long. My parents have kept me busy all day," Torin told Sneachta as he stroked its back between its small wings and placed another chunk of venison he had smuggled from the dinner table under Sneachta's nose. Sneachta gulped the meat down and burped again, but this time a small plume of smoke burst from Sneachta's nose. Torin was startled, and he jumped back, but then he laughed when Sneachta giggled. Sneachta reminded him of the dogs who always woofed down their meals like they were starving.

"I am feeling better now," Sneachta said. "I have to be leaving soon to return home."

"Do you know the way home?" Torin asked.

"From the sky I do," Sneachta replied.

Torin thought about Sneachta's answer. Of course, Sneachta was carried in the air, so he would see where he was going. "Can you fly?" Torin asked.

"Not yet, but soon I can," replied Sneachta, "I have to. I have to get home."

"I was thinking about that. Getting you home, that is," Torin said. "If we can find a good faerie, then maybe it could help you get home."

Sneachta thought about Torin's idea for a moment. "That might work," Sneachta said.

"Oh, I've been meaning to ask you, are you a boy or a girl dragon? It's hard to tell when you're so small," Torin asked.

"I'm a boy," Sneachta answered relieved Torin thought to ask instead of lifting him and looking under his tail. It was very embarrassing for a dragon. Sneachta liked Torin; he had respect for others and was very kind hearted.

Torin smiled, "A boy, huh? Just like me!" Suddenly Torin felt closer to the dragon. They were both young boys and in many ways still helpless against the big world.

"You're my new friend, Torin" said Sneachta, "Thank you."

Torin stroked Sneachta again and replied, "And you are my new friend. Together we will get you home."

Feigning exhaustion from doing so many chores that day, Torin told his parents he was going to bed early. Not trusting that Torin was really tired but coming down with something, Torin's mother, Maelíosa, checked him for a fever. Torin always did the same chores and never ran out of energy. Even though Torin didn't have a fever yet, his mother let him go to bed early just in case. Sleep would help fend off any sickness trying to spawn his mother thought. But just to be sure, Torin's mother made him drink a nasty tasting bitter herbal tea. Maelíosa was the valley's herbalist and medicine woman. She had a great talent for concocting cures for what ailed a person. Before Dorcha's dragon burned down the farm, she had a great greenhouse and vast gardens of herbs and other plants. Though she was slowly growing things back now, many plants had been lost, some that had been handed down to her from other medicine women, including her own mother. The rarest of the lost plants she could never find again. It would be a while yet before Torin's mother had regained her glorious gardens once more.

Though he resented having to drink the bitter tea, Torin understood his mother made him drink it because she loved him and worried about him. He felt guilty about what he was about to do. He knew it would cause his mother grief. Torin gave his mother a big hug and kissed her on her cheek. "I love you so much, Mom," Torin said, and then he turned to go to his room. Torin wanted his mother to know he loved her. He would be leaving after everyone was asleep, and he didn't know how long he would be gone. Maelíosa sat and looked at her son as he walked away. It almost seemed as if he was saying goodbye for some reason. But after a second or two, she brushed the thought off. He was just tired. It was winter now, and Torin had spent half the day in the cold barn. Perhaps he really was tired. She got up from her chair to concoct a new herbal formula for her family to get them through the cold season in better health.

When Torin went into his room instead of getting ready for bed, he took his backpack out from under his bed and started to supply it with things he thought he would need on his journey. He hoped it would be a short journey because he knew he would be in all kinds of trouble for it. But the alternative of watching Sneachta be destroyed and possibly stuffed by Alsandar was unbearable for Torin. He would rather take the punishment of his parents than see Sneachta suffer anymore. Once his backpack was as complete as he could make it, Torin went to bed. Other items he would have to sneak out after the rest of his family fell asleep. It wasn't long after Torin had gone to bed that his father looked in to see if he was doing okay and then some time after that, Maelíosa quietly crept in to check Torin for a fever again. As he felt her soft gentle hands caressing his head, Torin felt bad for betraying his mother, but it had to be done. Maelíosa bent down and kissed her son on his forehead and watched him for a few moments longer. Torin pretended he was asleep. When she finally left his room and closed his door Torin softly whispered after her, "I love you too, Mom."

When Torin felt sure the house was quiet and everyone else was asleep, he snuck down to the larder and stuffed food for the journey in his pack. It was heavy from all the venison he knew Sneachta needed, but he would carry it no matter what. Torin also knew his father would be furious; however, he decided to tuck the thought away until the time came when he would have to face his parents for his indiscretion. Laying his backpack aside, Torin snuck into Alsandar's room, and, in his mind, "borrowed" Alsandar's magic fire light. *I'm not really stealing it,* he thought to himself. He would be returning it when he came back, so it wasn't really stealing, just borrowing. He knew Alsandar would be quite upset with him, but Torin felt it was a necessary item, and he knew if he asked Alsandar for it, he would say no, and then, even worse, he would have to tell Alsandar why, and then it would all be over. Sneachta would end up patched back together again after his father hacked him to death with his sword and then stuffed sitting on a shelf in Alsandar's collection. He could not tell anyone why he was borrowing the magic fire light, but most importantly he needed it—it would give him light and warmth for his journey.

Chapter 3

The night air was snapping cold as Torin crept out of the house. As he breathed in the icy air, Torin could feel the hairs in his nose freeze. Sneachta was safely tucked inside Torin's winter coat where he would be warm and dry. As Torin walked a few paces, he suddenly realized Sneachta was a bit heavier than when he had first found him. He wondered how fast baby dragons grew. When Torin was far enough away from the house, he took out the magic fire light. Torin knew when Alsandar found out and saw him again, he would probably get a few smacks in the head after he yelled and screamed at him. But that could wait until after he had found a way to get Sneachta home. Alsandar didn't like anyone messing with his magic. Alsandar said more harm than good would come from it if you were not educated enough to use his magic things. The night was dark, and the moon was hidden behind the clouds. Torin could tell from the feel of the night air that it would start to snow again soon. The magic fire light would help light his way and keep him warm. Torin knew how to use that. He often watched his brother Alsandar practice his magic.

Not knowing where to start, Torin took Sneachta back to where he had found him. He dusted the snow off a rock and sat down opening his coat enough for Sneachta to pop his head out.

"I'm not sure where to go from here, Sneachta. Do you know where a good faerie might live?"

Sneachta yawned. He had fallen asleep in the warmth of Torin's coat. "Faeries like green places, where there are lots of growing things, trees, and water," Sneachta answered between yawns. Torin looked around. There were no green places or growing things in the cold season. All he saw was snow-covered ground, bare trees, and shrubs. The plants and grass had died down long ago and were covered in snow. Any water would be frozen. "They don't come out at all when it is cold," Sneachta added.

Torin's heart fell. "Why?" asked Torin.

"Because during winter everything is sleeping. They hide underground in winter caves or deep under the mud of ice-covered ponds and streams until spring," Sneachta answered. Torin wondered why Sneachta didn't say so before when he told him of his plan. It was going to be harder than he first thought it would be. After a bit of thought, Torin decided to find a pond or a lake. Maybe he could get their attention above the ice. Perhaps he could stir one up by banging on the ice or digging in to a faerie snow cave if he found the right spot.

"We need to find some water," Torin said.

"I saw a lake above the valley and over the mountain before I was dropped," Sneachta said.

"Then that is where we will look," Torin replied. Taking up the magic fire light to light the way, Torin rose. Following Sneachta's directions, the two set off to climb over the mountain to find the lake. Sneachta knew where he had traveled through the air. Sneachta would be his guide if they could follow the path on land.

As he walked, the only sound Torin heard was the crunching of the snow under his feet. He stopped for a moment to gaze upon the mountain he was about to climb, which made him feel very small and vulnerable. He was glad it was winter. Most wild creatures would be tucked away in hibernation. Still Torin kept his ears open for any sound at all just in case he had been discovered by a saber tooth or wyvern. He knew they at least still came out to hunt in the cold season. Being so small and young, he felt a little frightened about his journey. The thought of what could happen to Sneachta if he gave up compelled him on though. Sneachta's destruction would be harder to live with than the fear he now felt inside. Torin couldn't live with himself if he didn't try to help save Sneachta. Sneachta's presence gave him some comfort though even if he was still a small dragon. Torin was not alone. The warm body tucked beneath his winter coat reminded him of that. He hoped it would not take long to find a good faerie.

As Torin and Sneachta traveled up the side of the valley's edge, the wind whipped up with a frenzy, foretelling a fierce snowstorm was about to come again. From the dark silhouettes covering the side of the mountain, Torin knew it was a forest. If they could hurry and make it there soon, the trees would help protect them some from the snow and wind. He had learned a lot from his father on how to survive out in the wilderness. His father had taught him all he knew when he started to take his son out with him on his hunting trips. Torin's father knew that sometimes things could go wrong in the wilderness, and he wanted his sons to know what to do and how to survive. But Torin was still a small boy. He was only nine years old. His brothers were young men already. Micheál was tall and strong and knew just about everything. Alsandar was very cleaver and had his magic to help him through any problems. Torin wished he could have taken his brothers with him. But he thought they would not have come. In fact they would have just made things worse had he confided in them.

When Torin and Sneachta were halfway up the valley's edge, the snowstorm stopped. Feeling very tired, damp, and chilled, Torin wanted to find a safe hidden spot to take a nap, eat something, and, with the help of the magic fire light, dry out. He had not slept at all since the night before, and he knew he could not go much farther without some sleep. As he looked to the east, he saw the pre-dawn light on the edge of the horizon. It was almost dawn. Soon his family would be awake, and soon they would discover he was gone. The thought made Torin feel sick to his stomach. He knew his mom and dad would worry. But as soon as he found a good faerie to help Sneachta, he would return home. "We have to find a place to sleep, Sneachta. I am very tired!" Torin said. Sneachta poked his head out. His dragon eyes were far better than Torin's human eyes, and he could easily make out the terrain in the dark. After looking for another hour, Sneachta found a small crevice in the side of a slope under a rocky shelf. Taking branches of pine trees and any other things he could find, Torin built a cover over the crevice to hide its entrance. Once inside and with the magic fire light to keep him warm, Torin curled up on the hard ground and instantly fell asleep. The sun had already peaked above the horizon. Sneachta kept watch as he had already slept most the way in Torin's warm coat.

Chapter 4

Maelíosa had the hearth fire blazing as she prepared the morning breakfast for her family. Though it was noon already, her family had been too busy out looking for Torin to start breakfast until then. Her grief and worry consumed her thoughts. She had risen early to check on her son to make sure he was doing okay and wasn't ill as she previously thought, but Torin was gone. She searched the house, the barn, and everywhere she could think of, but there was no sign of her son. It had snowed a great deal during the night, and all tracks he might have made were gone. She thought about the kiss and hug she had received from her son the night before. It had seemed to her as if he was saying goodbye. Why didn't she listen to her gut feelings? As she held the iron pan in her hands to start the meal preparation, she threw it against the wall and sat down in a chair and cried.

Torin's father felt absolute panic in his mind. His heart ached for his son. He felt responsible for Torin's disappearance. He had failed to protect his family. He tried to remain calm and strong for the rest of his family, but the loss of his son was beginning to overwhelm him. He had been out for hours with his older sons looking for little Torin, but there was no sign of him. There were no tracks to follow or any sign of where he had gone. The nighttime snowstorm had erased all clues. Little Torin had just vanished in the night. Ernst decided to go to the village and ask around. Perhaps he could get more people in on the search. Sending his other son's home to comfort his wife and wait in case Torin showed up, Ernst told them he would get people from the village to help and to let their mother know.

Once back home Micheál and Alsandar found their mother in a kitchen chair staring at a wall. The hearth was blazing, and an iron pan sat on the floor under a dent in the wall. Maelíosa's face was puffy, and her eyes were red and swollen. They knew she had been crying. Micheál went to the wall and picked up the pan. Stopping to kiss his mother on the top of her head, he said, "It will be okay, Mom. We'll find Torin." Micheál then told her what his father said and started to fix something for them to eat. Alsandar stayed by his mother's side holding her in his arms.

"Don't worry, Mom. Torin will be just fine. Dad taught him a lot of things to keep safe out there," Alsandar said trying to comfort his mother. He felt her grief as well as his own.

Alsandar thought of his little brother. He never did pay as much attention to him as he should have. Little Torin always seemed to be in his way, asking questions and messing with his magic things while he tried to practice. At the time it seemed annoying to Alsandar. If little Torin came back, Alsandar decided he would be more patient. Perhaps his little brother had a natural talent like he did for magic. He would teach little Torin what he had learned. And then it dawned on Alsandar: he could use his magic to help find his brother!

After they had eaten, the two brothers watched as their mother picked at her food, occasionally wiping a lose tear from her eyes. "Mom, I'm going to use my magic to help find Torin. I know I can do it," Alsandar told his mother.

Maelíosa looked up. "Of course! Why didn't we think of that before?" she asked. Jumping up, she ran to Torin's room. The brothers followed her. Reaching in his dirty clothes basket she handed a shirt to Alsandar. "Can you use this to find out where he went?"

"Maybe," Alsandar replied. He took the shirt and went to his room in the attic followed by his brother and mother. Drawing a magic circle on the floor and chanting a spell of insight and protection, Alsandar placed the shirt and a chalice of holy water in the center. As Alsandar chanted asking for his brother's location, the three watched as an image of Torin grew in the waters center. There they saw him during his previous hunting trip pick up something long and white and put it in his coat. Then the image changed as a great black dragon roared, and a large black raven with the head of a woman laughing wickedly flew away. The water then changed back to normal.

Maelíosa sat back on her heals, wondering what it was she had just seen. She recognized the black dragon as Dorcha's dragon. That was something she would never forget. She remembered the nights of terror running with her family to get away from the fire spewing out of the great beast's mouth, consuming everything around them, hoping the dragon would not swoop down and eat them. Little Torin had been just a toddler then. She had him wrapped tightly in her arms as she ran.

"What does that mean? What does little Torin have to do with Dorcha and her dragon?" Maelíosa asked.

"And what is that raven all about?" Micheál added. "Was that Dorcha?"

Alsandar didn't answer at first. He had to think of what he had just seen. Dorcha's dragon was gone, but Dorcha was still around. Though after the winter queen's punishment, no one had heard from or seen Dorcha since. And the white thing Torin had picked up, what was that? Then he remembered. "Micheál! Do you remember that dying lizard Torin wanted to bring home during our last hunting trip with him?" Alsandar asked.

"Yes, that's right. Dad told him no," Micheál answered.

"But he did it anyway." Alsandar replied.

Maelíosa stood up and asked, "What lizard?"

Alsandar ran to little Torin's room, and the other two followed behind him wondering what it was all about. After a few minutes of searching, Alsandar found the niche in the wall and pulled out the box with Torin's old shirt still in it. It had a funny smell. Then Torin saw it—droppings from its inhabitant. Micheál took the box and smelled it, too. "I've smelled that before!" he said. The two boys looked at each other.

Maelíosa, being impatient to hear what they had found, yelled, "What! What is it?" as she looked anxiously back and forth at her two sons.

Alsandar replied, "That wasn't a lizard Torin brought home. It was a dragon!" Maelíosa was stunned. A dragon! Why did he bring home a dragon? She sat on the edge of Torin's bed and looked at her sons. She didn't know where to begin with her questions. As the images from Alsandar's magic spell ran through her mind, all kinds of possibilities came to her, and none of them were good ones.

Micheál explained to his mother what had happened on his last hunting trip. They didn't think Torin would disobey his father and bring the lizard home. But Maelíosa knew her son. He was always saving creatures and had a kind heart. Little Torin didn't like to see anything suffer. "So what does that dragon have to do with Dorcha's dragon?" Maelíosa asked. No one had an answer at first.

After a few moments of silence, Alsandar said what he didn't want to say: "Maybe it was Dorcha's new dragon, and she found out Torin had it?" Maelíosa felt sheer terror race through her chest. If Dorcha had her son, she would never get him back again. Once a human was taken to the realm of night, they never came back. On the rare occasions they did return, they could not stand the daylight, and then they had been changed. They were never human again.

After seeing the look of terror on his mother's face, Micheál glared at Alsandar. Trying to spare his mother further grief, Micheál racked his memory to find reasons why Alsandar's comment couldn't be true. Going back over what he had learned when he was studying to be a dragoneer, Micheál explained why he didn't think it could be Dorcha's dragon after all. "I don't think Dorcha would have a white dragon, Alsandar. White dragons are rare and very powerful. Dorcha is a powerful faerie, but she isn't a grand faerie. She could not handle that kind of dragon. White dragons only chose to be with the elemental faeries that are more powerful, and Dorcha is a night faerie. She deals more with emotions than elements."

Maelíosa felt some relief, but that still didn't explain where her son was or how they would find him or what Dorcha's dragon had to do with it all. Alsandar felt a growing sense that something was out of place with all of what was taking place. Dorcha was involved somehow, but he agreed with his older brother. The white dragon wasn't Dorcha's. So what was her part in all this? Could she have taken Torin anyway because he did have a white dragon? He didn't think that was the answer. Maybe she had tried to kill it or something and Torin took the dragon and ran? *At least he could have left a note or something!* Alsandar chided in his head. Whatever the truth was, Alsandar knew Torin was in danger, and he had to be found as soon as possible! "Don't you worry, Mom! I'm going to get Torin back!" Alsandar said. "Let's go, Micheál."

As the two brothers left the room, Micheál called back to his mom, "I know it's hard, but you have to stay here in case little Torin comes back. And let Dad know what we have found out."

Taking Torin's pillow in her arms, Maelíosa hugged it and took in his scent. Deep down she was comforted by the feeling that she was sure her other sons would find her missing son. Between Micheál's strength and courage and Alsandar's determination and magic, they would succeed. But most of all, she knew love would find a way to bring her son back to her. However, the waiting would be unbearable. She didn't want to stay behind doing nothing but waiting. That was the hardest part of all. The others would be occupied with doing something. She wondered how she could survive it all.

While Micheál went to his room to pack anything he thought he might need for what may be a long journey, Alsandar went to the attic and gathered any magic items and emergency spells he would need. But when he went to get his magic fire light, he found it was gone. Stumped as to where it could have gone, he searched and searched. Alsandar couldn't find it. Taking out his wand, he chanted his reveal-spell for missing and lost items, and there in the smoky mist at the end of his wand he saw his little brother, Torin, taking it. At first he was angry, but then he remembered his promise to himself to be more patient with his little brother. Alsandar was relieved that Torin had at least one magic item that would help him survive. But then Alsandar had an idea. If his spell could work for minor things, perhaps he could find a way for it to work on bigger things like people. It would take time to come up with that one. He grabbed his encyclopedia of sorcerers' spells and stuffed it in his backpack. He didn't have time to look for a new spell, and with the book, he could look as they searched. The sooner the brothers were on their way, the sooner they could get Torin back before something really terrible happened.

Once outside, the brothers stood wondering what direction to go in. Alsandar had another idea spring to his mind. Taking out his wand, he chanted his spell for lost items, but this time he asked for when the magic fire light was last used. At the tip of his wand, the red smoky plume came out showing Torin standing where they were now standing. Then it changed again and again at various places until it came to the location of where Torin had first found the white lizard and then finally what looked to be a pine forest in the dark. "We can use the fire light to track him," Alsandar said.

"Good work!" Micheál replied. He ran back into the house to tell his mother so she could tell their father where the trail began. Maelíosa grabbed her coat and said goodbye to her sons as she went to the barn to get a horse to ride to the village. Her heart soared with joy. She felt sure her boys would soon bring Torin home. The two brothers then set off in the direction of the dragon find. She wished they had more horses again; her sons could travel faster that way. But Dorcha's dragon had destroyed them, and they had only managed to get by with two horses so far, and the other one was with her husband. Feeling hope rise deep within her heart, Maelíosa hopped on her horse and galloped to the village to tell her husband what had happened.

Chapter 5

By the time Micheál and Alsandar had started to climb the valley edge following their little brother's trail up the mountain, the snow began to fall again. Micheál stopped to sniff the air. "What is it?" Alsandar asked.

"I think a blizzard is coming," Micheál replied. "We need to find a place to hunker down for a bit and quick." Alsandar was amazed by his older brother's ability to guess the weather. He always knew when a storm was coming and how bad or easy it would be. Sometimes Alsandar wondered if Micheál had a bit of faerie blood in him. Not being able to find a cave or natural niche to wait out the blizzard in, with the help of Alsandar's magic, the two brothers quickly built a shelter under a stand of pine trees. Using his magic once more, Alsandar had a nice fire going to keep them warm while they waited for the snowstorm to blow through. The two sat in silent disappointment. The storm would put the hunt on hold for a bit, and they hoped Torin had the sense to find shelter as well. Meanwhile the rescue party Ernst had put together had to wait the storm out at his farm. But though the blizzard was blowing hard by then, they had great hope with the news a trail had been found. Maelíosa happily set a hot meal out for those who came to help. She had high hopes and felt a deep sense of faith that eventually little Torin would be home again.

Sneachta had gone out to relieve himself when he felt the air change. A blizzard was coming. He scampered back into the niche where little Torin was sleeping. He decided not to wake him. Maybe Torin would just sleep through the storm, and so it wouldn't matter at all anyway. Torin did just that; he slept through the storm. The wind howled, and the makeshift shelter rattled for a while until enough snow had covered it to hold it down steady. Little Torin was so tired that he slept through it all. The magic fire lights glow kept him warm and snug.

After the winter storm had spent its energy, Torin woke up. Sneachta was curled up next to his head. "There was a blizzard while you slept," Sneachta said. "We are buried in the snow." Torin sat up and looked around. He had forgotten where he was for the moment.

"That's ok. We'll dig our way out," Torin replied as he grabbed his backpack and took out something for the two of them to eat. Torin wasn't worried; he knew he could dig a tunnel out. He had spent many winters making and digging tunnels in the snow with his older brothers. He gave Sneachta a piece of raw venison and toasted his own over the magic fire light and made a sandwich out of it with a couple of pieces of the bread he had taken from his mother's larder. He thought of her while he savored the taste of her home-cooked bread with each bite. They would know he was gone by now. Torin thought of his mother and father. "I love you!" Torin quietly whispered to himself sending out his thoughts to his parents.

Having filled their bellies, Torin and Sneachta dug their way out into the snowy daylight. Torin laughed as he watched Sneachta scamper and roll in the snow. Digging their way out of the shelter had been easy, and the two stopped for a moment to play. Torin made a little snow man and taught Sneachta how to make snow angels. Sneachta was happy with his new friend, and the two enjoyed their short play time in the winter landscape before moving on to find a good faerie. Up they climbed until the two had reached the mountain top. As Torin looked down, he could see for miles. Far off in the distance down below, he could see the lake surrounded by the forest. He had slept for half a day, and it would be dark again in a few hours. He decided to make his way toward the lake, covering as much ground as possible. He wished he had brought skis. In some places the snow was very, very deep and hard to walk through, and it was hard to see where it was easiest to walk.

Growing tired of trudging through the deep snow, Torin decided to look for something he could use as a sled. He tried weaving tree branches together, but it didn't work out very well, and he was wasting time in the process. Then as he decided to give up, he heard a low growl in the near distance. Startled, he looked around but could see nothing. He listened again. This time the growl was louder, and Torin knew it was the growl of a great cat. But since he couldn't see it, he didn't know what kind of great cat it was. Sneachta ran up Torin's leg and crawled into his coat. "What is it?" Sneachta squeaked.

"I'm not sure. It sounds like a panther or a saber tooth," replied Torin. Looking around, he saw a broken-up old tree a few feet away in a ruble of boulders. He ran to them and pulled out as much debris as he could in piles, building an arc around him with his back to the boulders and ruble. Torin then lit the debris piles on fire with the magic fire light. The growl was coming closer, and then, as he stood behind the wall of flames, in front of him several feet away, he saw a large gray- and white-striped saber tooth cat slowly creeping toward him. The large saber tooth was crouched lowly like a barn cat sneaking up on its prey as it came slowly toward him with a low rumbling growl.

Hoping the flames would hold it back, Torin stood with the magic fire light in his hand. The saber tooth cat crept closer, ready to pounce, but the fire held it back. Torin's eyes grew wide in fear as he saw the powerful muscles of the saber tooth flexing with each movement under its striped fur. The great cat was large, very large, bigger than he was times six. The saber teeth of the cat jutted out like great swords curved downward. Torin could feel the power emanating from the great beast. He felt his legs shaking. He wondered if his family would ever know what happened to him. He felt his heart break as he yearned to be in the protective arms of his mother far away from the fear and madness he now felt inside.

With a low menacing growl still rumbling in its throat, the great cat started to pace back and forth, trying to find a way past the fire. Torin quickly lit several more pieces of old wood to form a solid wall. He then picked up a large rock and threw it at the great cat hitting him in the head. The great cat recoiled and roared in pain as blood flowed down his head. Torin gasped as he saw down the throat of the saber tooth and the rows of large sharp teeth he knew soon would be crunching on his flesh and bones. The cat was not about to give up even after Torin's attack. Hunger drove the cat on. Not even the fire could keep the great cat back. It wasn't about to give up on this seemingly easy catch. Slowly, the great cat crept right up to the fire and looked past it into Torin's eyes. As Torin stood eye to eye with the saber tooth, staring into its golden irises, somewhere deep inside Torin felt a sudden burst of courage. It was as if he could feel the strength, confidence, and determination of the great cat himself. He got as close as he could to the great cat on the other side of his fire wall and shouted, "Fire on the cat!" while he held the magic fire light out in front of him. The flames from the magic fire light shot out and engulfed the saber tooth cat. Screaming and howling in agony, the great cat took off running and stumbling and then rolling in the snow and running again as its fur burned. Sneachta poked his head out of Torin's coat.

"I bet he never messes with a human who has fire again," Sneachta said.

Torin watched as the saber tooth disappeared into the forest. "I bet!" he replied.

Torin sat down on a small boulder and thought just how silly he had been to think he could make his way safely through the wilderness to find a good faerie. Still shaking from his traumatic ordeal and thankful for his miraculous escape, he wondered if he should turn back as he fiddled with the edge of broken tree trunk that was lodged between the boulders. Looking down at the piece of tree trunk, he saw it was cracked, and the outer edge of the tree rings could easily break apart from its core. It would make a perfect sled! After a bit of struggling, Torin managed to push aside the boulder he had been sitting on, and the trunk fell. As it fell it broke into pieces, leaving a hollowed-out outer trunk that was just big enough for him to sit upon. Excited about the find, Torin quickly forgot he was thinking of turning back. Torin dragged the hull to the edge of the mountain and looked down toward the lake. Torin and Sneachta climbed on. Torin then pushed the makeshift sled off. As the two sped down the side of the mountain toward the lake, Sneachta came out of Torin's jacket just enough to lean on the front of the sled and enjoy the wind in his face. His long tongue hung out, wagging in the breeze and splattering Torin in the face occasionally with windblown saliva. With the makeshift sled, the two would be at the lake in no time at all.

Chapter 6

As the sun was starting to set, Micheál and Alsandar came upon Torin's shelter. They looked down on the snow-covered ground and found the tunnel, two snow angels, a small snowman, and wiggly lines and patches where it looked like something small rolled around in the snow making a very pathetic looking snow angel. And then they saw Torin's tracks that led off up to the mountain top. "Should we follow or make camp here?" Alsandar asked. Micheál looked at the setting sun. He wanted to follow Torin's tracks, but he knew continuing on in the dark and possibly getting caught in another snowstorm would be disastrous.

"We should probably stay here for the night. Torin is most likely doing the same thing wherever he is," Micheál said.

"But it might snow again, and then we would lose his tracks," Alsandar replied.

"True, but if there is another blizzard during the night, we would be caught out in it, and, besides, you can track him through the magic fire light."

Alsandar wasn't happy with Micheál's reply. He knew Micheál was right, but they were much closer now, and he didn't want to stop. Alsandar felt sure Torin was close within their reach. He decided to ignore Micheál's wisdom and started to follow Torin's tracks. Micheál called after Alsandar to come back and wait, but

Alsandar refused to listen. Torin was so close now, and he was determined to get to him quickly. Micheál followed and tackled him in the snow. "Get off me!" Alsandar yelled full of anger at his brother.

"Look! I want to follow him as much as you do, but getting ourselves killed won't do any good for anyone!" Micheál yelled back at his brother. Alsandar relented as he looked in his brothers' eyes. Alsandar knew Micheál was right. They already had one lost brother; the family didn't need the rest of them lost as well. Following Torin in the night could be hazardous. Between the wild animals and potential snowstorms, it was safer to stay put. The brothers got up from the wet ground, brushing off the snow. Alsandar picked up a handful of snow and shoved it down the neck of Micheál's coat. He was still angry at Micheál, even more so for being right. Micheál shoved Alsandar down in the snow again and turned toward the opening of Torin's tunnel. Alsandar sat in the snow for a few moments glaring at Micheál. Micheál offered his hand to Alsandar. After helping him up, they silently crawled into Torin's shelter for the night. Both were tired and angry that they had come so close yet had to fall behind again by waiting for morning's light. It was a small, cramped place for the two larger boys.

Breaking the silence, Alsandar managed a positive comment on Torin's small haven. "You know, he was very cleaver with this place."

"Yes, it's a good shelter; I think Torin will be all right for the night," Micheál said.

Alsandar woke first since his older brother, who was much larger than he was, had jabbed a knee in his stomach. Nudging his brother away, Alsandar leaned up and peered through the tunnel. There was no light. Taking out his wand and using it for a light to check his magic timekeeper, Alsandar saw it was still early. The hand was just a sliver from the rising sun on the face of his magic time piece. The sun would be up soon. Alsandar thought they had delayed enough; he didn't want to wait for sun rise. Crawling over his older brother, Alsandar went out into the snow. Though it was still dark out, Alsandar could see the thin sliver of dawn on the horizon. Using his wand again for a source of light, he examined the ground. He could still see the snow angels. It had snowed lightly in the night, but the tracks were still there.

"Micheál! Wake up!" Alsandar called through the snow tunnel. He then started a small fire to cook some smoked venison and warm the bread for their morning breakfast. Micheál crawled out of the tunnel still half asleep and sat down beside Alsandar. But not being fully awake yet, he fell back, and when he reached to catch himself, his hand landed in something slimy.

"*Eww!*" Micheál exclaimed. Alsandar watched as Micheál looked at what was smeared all over his hand. As he looked and sniffed to determine what it was, Micheál turned his nose up and whined. "Dragon Poo!" he lamented. Alsandar laughed.

"You know, that is actually a good thing," Alsandar said.

Feeling grumpy at such a rude awakening, Micheál asked, "And how is having dragon poo smeared all over my hand a good thing?"

Still laughing, Alsandar replied, "Because animals are afraid of dragons, and if they smell dragon poo, they won't come near you." Micheál shrugged and wiped the poo off on his coat.

"Maybe that is why Torin has gotten as far as he has," Micheál said. "He has a dragon with him."

The brothers followed Torin's trail using Alsandar's magic wand as a torch. The red glow at the end of its tip gave off ample light. After the sun had finally peaked over the horizon, the brothers came upon large animal tracks. Micheál examined them, then suddenly he exclaimed, "*Oh* Jeez!" Alsandar stood looking at the large tracks as well. The paw prints were much larger than a panther, but, worst of all, they were following Torin's tracks. "A saber tooth!" Micheál gasped. Alsandar felt his stomach turn. Panic took over his thoughts. Neither of the brothers could bear the thought of Torin being eaten by a saber tooth. The boys took off running following the tracks. Their hearts beat heavily as fear tinged the lining of their emotions. For quite some time, they followed the tracks, hoping with all their hearts there would be no blood trails or signs of a bloody struggle. Breaking through a particularly thick stand of pine trees, they saw the rubble of boulders and dead tree. There in front was a half-circle of burnt branches and logs.

The saber tooth's tracks followed over Torin's footprints in the snow. As the brothers came closer to the end of their trail, they saw the tracks of the saber tooth went back and forth in front of the burned-out barrier Torin had made. Micheál and Alsandar frantically looked over the prints in the snow trying to decipher their meaning. Several patches of crimson blood stood out marking the white snow. Next to one of the blood patches laid a bloody rock. As Micheál looked further, he saw something he didn't want to see. Something large had been dragged in the snow. Alsandar watched Micheál. *What was it?* Alsandar thought. Did this mean Torin was dragged away? After a few moments of thought Micheál stopped walking around and stood with his hands on his hips "This doesn't make sense." Micheál said.

"What doesn't make sense?" Alsandar asked, wondering if there was anything to hope for.

"Look, something was dragged away in that direction and then in the opposite direction you can see the saber tooth's tracks." Micheál replied as he pointed in the two different directions. Alsandar looked and saw the saber tooth's tracks led away from the other. Micheál followed the big cats trail and decided the blood came from the cat.

"Do you think there was another cat?" Alsandar asked.

"No, there's only one set of animal tracks here Alsandar." Micheál answered. Alsandar followed the drag marks in the snow. Then he saw it! Footprints, human footprints!

"Micheál come look at this!" Alsandar shouted, "I think he got away!"

"Looks like he was dragging something." Micheál said. The brothers followed the trail in the snow up the slope where they saw Deiter's footprints all around the flat object he had dragged and then vanished leaving only a smooth indentation in the snow that went down the mountain hill below.

"You know, he's a lot smarter than we ever gave him credit for," Alsandar said, looking down the path of Torin's sled track.

"Yup!" Micheál replied, his heart greatly relieved that it looked as if Torin had gotten away from the saber tooth. Looking around at what was left of the dead tree, Alsandar took out his encyclopedia of magic. "What's that for?" Micheál asked.

"I'm looking for something I can use to turn this jumble of dead tree trash into a sled. It looks like Torin took the best part."

"Well, hurry up. With that sled, Torin will be getting a lot farther away a lot faster," Micheál said. Alsandar instructed Micheál to put as many pieces of dead wood together as he could find to form the shape of a sled large enough for the two of them. Using thin, willowy tree branches, Micheál laid them out to form a line like rope and smaller pieces of the dead tree for a steering mechanism. By the time he had finished, Alsandar had put together a spell that would bind all the pieces of wood together in one shape and form the parts he wanted. After about an hour, the sled was complete. The two brothers hopped on and followed Torin's path down the mountain toward the lake. Alsandar made Micheál sit behind him so he would be up-wind of Micheál's newly acquired dragon-poo scent. They had not been long on their journey down when the brothers passed a curious sight. Upon a ledge sat a strange-looking beast with saber teeth. It had no fur with funny looking stumpy ears and was busy licking red and black patches on its hairless skin. Upon seeing the brothers go by on their magic sled, it screamed out in great fear and ran away.

Chapter 7

Torin had arrived at the lake by late afternoon. Both he and Sneachta searched and searched in the bushes, shrubs, alcoves, and silent frozen edges of reeds, hoping they would find some clue of a good faerie's presence. When the sun had finally dipped to the very edge of the horizon, he gave up for the night and built a simple shelter to sleep in under the low branches of a fir tree. While Sneachta was sleeping, curled up in Torin's jacket, and Torin was sound asleep far away in dreamland, a strange wind blew outside the shelter around the lake. Neither heard the cries of the wind, "Sneachta, Sneachta, where are you?" The ground gave up its snow in flurries followed by another blizzard that followed in the wind's wake and then died down as the cries of the strange wind vanished in the distance. Neither the winter queen nor Sneachta had realized just how close they had come to finding each other.

The next morning Sneachta and Torin began looking again. They called out for any good faeries that might be there and dug in crevices under shrubs and bushes just in case they were too deep down to hear them calling. Torin and Sneachta had even gone out on the frozen lake to look under the ice in case any water nymphs might be there who could help them. Torin had even punched a hole in the ice and called down into the water, but it was all to no avail. They just were not coming out in the cold season. Just as they were about to give up and travel on again, Torin suddenly heard a loud "Wahoo!" and as he turned to see what it was, he was instantly caught up by his brother Micheál as their sled swooshed by and came to a crashing stop in a bramble bush. All three brothers were tossed in the air, landing jumbled in the snow. Startled, Sneachta ran over to see what all the commotion was about and if his new friend Torin was all right. "Torin, you little toad!" Alsandar cried out as the brothers got up and then wrestled him into the snowy ground.

"Why?" asked Micheál. Freeing himself from his brothers' grasp, Torin got up, brushing the snow off his face and shoulders. He said nothing. He didn't know where to begin, and seeing his older brothers suddenly appear out of nowhere and throw him on the ground threw his ability to think clearly off. "Mom and Dad are sick with worry over you!" scolded Micheál.

"Torin, is you all right?" Sneachta called as he scrambled up Torin's body and around his neck. Sneachta grabbed on to Torin's ears with his little claws and looked him over as if he were a doctor looking for wounds. Turning to the brothers, Sneachta scolded them. "What are you doing? You bad boys, you could have hurt my friend!" Alsandar and Micheál were startled. "Wow! Just look at him, Alsandar. It's the dragon!" Micheál exclaimed, thrilled to see one so up close.

"It's a real dragon!" Alsandar replied, looking closely at Sneachta with his mouth open in awe.

Pulling Sneachta gently off his ears, Torin introduced him to his brothers. "This is Sneachta. I am helping him find his way home again."

Still surprised at seeing a baby dragon so close up, Alsandar asked, "Why?"

"Yeah, why, and why didn't you say anything? You just up and left without saying a word to anyone!" Micheál scolded.

"Because," Torin said, "you just would have killed him, and Alsandar would have stuffed him as one of his weird trophies for his magic and stuff. And Mom and Dad would have said no, I couldn't keep him or help him." Torin started to cry. "He's just a boy, a boy like me who wants to go home." Then he looked up at his brothers with anger burning in his eyes. "Besides, you all hate dragons! You wouldn't have helped us!" Torin yelled. With Torin's last words, Sneachta's anger turned to fear. Would they kill and stuff him like Torin had just said? He crawled down into Torin's jacket and curled up in a tight ball and started to cry. He would never get home now, and he would never see his beloved Aunt Geal again.

The three brothers stood in silence. Alsandar thought about Torin's accusation. He did have thoughts of stuffing the white lizard. It was an unusual lizard, and Alsandar had thought it would be a unique addition to his collection of unusual things. It would have looked quite handsome next to his stuffed two headed squirrel. Micheál admitted to himself there had been days in the past when he would like nothing more than all dragons to have vanished from the face of the earth. He was old enough to remember quite well the night of terror when Droch completely destroyed his home. Micheál subconsciously rubbed the scars that lie under his sleeves and coat. His arm had been severely burnt that night. As he stood face to face with the little white dragon that was peeking out at him from Torin's coat Micheál imagined what it would be like when full grown and powerful. He knew the full pyrotechnic capabilities the little creature in his brother's protection would be capable of some day. If ever there was an easy time to kill a dragon, now would be the time when it was still small and vulnerable.

Alsandar looked at the dragon again. It was so alive now. It looked nothing like it did when he first saw it lying lifeless in the snow. It had grown quite a bit larger now as well. Alsandar knew deep down he could never kill and stuff such a beast. He never killed except for self defense and hunger. But this creature was no threat to him nor was it at deaths door. Alsandar really didn't want to stuff Sneachta. It was only when he thought the strange lizard was dead he would stuff him. And he did like some dragons; he just hated Dorcha and her evil dragon. He was an apprentice sorcerer, after all, and dragons and other strange beasts were all part of his world.

Micheál had never talked to anyone about his feelings since that awful night. He just went with the flow. But now here was a dragon, a real living breathing dragon right in front of him. He saw the care and affection the dragon held for his little brother and how Torin went to such great lengths to care and protect the dragon in return. He thought of all the hours in the past he had studied dragons and dreamed of working with them someday. Micheál suddenly realized that not all dragons are bad dragons. Deep inside Micheál felt excited about being so close to a dragon. He wished it had been he who stood there with a dragon in his coat instead of his little brother. Micheál finally realized that when faced with the truth he still liked dragons. Micheál took Torin under his arm and held him until his tears stopped flowing. Micheál understood why it all had happened. No one talked about their real feelings to anyone, especially the dark days of Droch's reign of terror. Everyone just hid what they really felt from each other. It was no wonder Torin had misunderstood them all.

"Torin, no one wants to kill and stuff Sneachta," Micheál gently said. Then looking at his brother Alsandar, Micheál sternly added, "Isn't that right, Alsandar!"

Being quick to reply Alsandar said, "Oh, no! Never. I like dragons!" Shrugging and kicking a bit of snow with his toe, Alsandar explained why he wanted to stuff Sneachta. "It's just that I thought he was pretty much dead and beyond hope, Torin. I would never kill and stuff a creature like that, unless of course it was a saber tooth or grisly or something that was trying to kill me."

"If you had just trusted us, we might have been able to help you Torin," Micheál said.

"But as far as Mom and Dad go? I agree with you on them. They would not have had anything to do with a dragon, that's for sure," Alsandar said.

"Well, I'm starved. Let's eat and then think of what to do next," Micheál said.

Micheál built a small woodpile for a fire, and Torin showed them how he thwarted the saber tooth cat by lighting the woodpile with a command to the magic fire light. Alsandar was impressed. It had taken him several days to build up his faith strong enough to make it shoot fire. But in Torin's case, necessity brought forth his faith in one attempt. Magic was all about faith. Faith was the energy behind every spell and magical command. Faith moved mountains. It changed matter and circumstances. It was faith that had brought Torin and Sneachta this far, and it was faith that allowed Micheál and Alsandar to find their little brother.

Torin felt much better now about things. He was also happy his big brothers were there with him. He felt much safer, and his world became suddenly more secure in their presence. After finishing his last bite, Torin was eager to know what his big brothers had planned for Sneachta. "So what are you going to do now?" Torin asked. Sneachta stuck his head out of Torin's coat and looked at the older boys. He wanted to know too. Their decision might mean he would be abandoned to find his way home on his own. For with or without help from his friend, he would continue on. He hoped Torin would still be able to help him; he didn't want to say goodbye to him.

Micheál put his sandwich of smoked venison down on his backpack. He chuckled as he looked over at Sneachta, who was looking at him. The baby dragon looked so cute, yet serious, as he poked out from Torin's coat. With a big warm smile Micheál said, "Come here, Sneachta." Sneachta hesitated. He didn't know if he should trust the older boy. Alsandar giggled and reached up and stroked Sneachta's head.

"It's okay, Sneachta, we won't hurt you. We like you," Alsandar said. Torin smiled at his brothers, and Sneachta decided that was enough for trust. Sneachta came out and jumped into Micheál's outstretched hand. Micheál drew him closer and held him in his arms and stroked his scaly back between his wings.

"I don't know what we should do exactly, but I think we should find a way to help this dragon get home." Micheál said. Micheál had been thinking about his brother and his words spoken through his tears "He's just a boy like me who wants to go home." If they had not been able to find Torin, and someone else had, he hoped they would help him find his way home as well.

"Mom and Dad will be real mad at us, Micheál," Alsandar said.

"I know, but if it was Torin who was lost, would you want someone to help him find his way home? I think Mom and Dad would want the same thing, too."

While they sat around the fire after their meal, Sneachta told the older brothers how he had gotten lost in the woods and taken by a large raven. Sneachta also told them that he could find his way home by what he remembered from the air, and that it might be enough to find their way from the ground. After listening to Sneachta's story, Alsandar had another idea. Looking through his encyclopedia of sorcerer's spells, he put another one on the magic sled that would help them find their way by air. Micheál knew his father would follow their trail, as the boys had left red twine tied to tree branches just in case they got lost, as well. Taking out his notebook, Alsandar left a note for his father. "Dear Dad, found Torin, he is fine. He was helping a lost boy find his way home. We are going to help. Be home soon and don't worry, we are okay. Alsandar, Micheál, and Torin."

Chapter 8

Ernst stood by the lake, reading the note Alsandar had left for him. He didn't know what to think of it. The note didn't tell him very much. He was relieved to know that little Torin was okay and with his older brothers. He wished he knew where they were going though and who it was they were helping. Maelíosa had told him about the baby dragon and the vision Alsandar had conjured. Ernst realized the mysterious boy was probably the baby dragon. It must be a very special dragon. It had been a white dragon, and the only white dragon Ernst knew of belonged to the winter queen. Maybe it was her dragon? Returning it home would certainly be the right thing to do, especially after all the winter queen had done for the people of the Valley of the Dragon. Even so, Ernst disliked the idea of his son's getting too close to the realm of a faerie. He knew how dangerous it could be. It worried him greatly.

Ernst could not understand why Torin would just take off like that in the middle of the night and not say a word. As Ernst looked back at the day he told his son to just leave the lizard and get along home, he felt immense regret. If he had just stopped and listened and looked instead of being temperamental, he could have saved his family a great deal of pain and suffering. The whole family could have helped return the dragon back to the winter queen if it was her dragon and little Torin would have been safe and sound from the beginning. But what worried him the most was why Dorcha and her black dragon were involved. If the white dragon was lost because of her, then all three of his boys would be in danger. That was something he could not live with. But for now all he could do was return home and wait and hope. The trail his sons had left stopped cold. There were no more tracks leading anywhere, and he didn't know where the winter queen lived to ask her for help. No mortal did. The faeries kept themselves hidden from the world of men, and those who did find out never came back again. He hoped the winter queen would be benevolent once more and return his sons.

The boy's had left tracks and evidence in the snow they had been there, but then suddenly they had vanished. There were no tracks leading from the site anywhere to follow. With no further tracks to follow and no clues to which direction his son's went, Ernst and his search party turned back for home. They would have to just sit and wait until they heard further news. At least he could bring some hope and a kind of peace home to his wife with this news. Sadly, Ernst got back on his horse, and the search party returned home with heavy hearts.

Once again Sneachta stood at the helm of the sled as it flew through the air over the forest below, his tongue wagging in the wind, splattering Torin and Alsandar with saliva. Micheál had again been asked to sit last on the sled downwind due to his smell. Alsandar had come through again with his encyclopedia of magic. He had managed to cast a flight spell on the sled. But though it didn't fly very high with all three boys on the sled, it flew high enough over the trees, nonetheless, and Sneachta was able to navigate the way home easier. While the brothers were busy laughing and enjoying the ride and Sneachta was gleefully pretending he was flying on his own, none of them noticed a large winged creature quickly descending upon them from behind. As soon as they heard the screech of the large raven, it was too late. A bright flash of dark blue light surged toward them. The sled was hit and shattered in the air. The brothers and Sneachta fell toward the canopy of pines and barren trees below. All Sneachta could think of was, *Not again!* as he grasped Torin's coat tightly and crawled inside.

As the brothers hit the treetops, Alsandar was glad Micheál had insisted they all be tied together in case someone fell off. Though the jolt was painful as they hit the branches, the treetops also buffered the fall and made the crash to the ground a great deal safer. The brothers were still tied together with Micheál hanging from a lower branch dangling Torin on one side and Alsandar on the other from the rope.

"Is everyone alright?" Alsandar asked as he examined a long cut on his hand.

"I don't know. My stomach hurts," replied Micheál. Struggling, Alsandar distorted his body to undo his backpack. Trying not to spill anything from within the pack because of his precarious dangling position, Alsandar reached in to get his knife. After he cut Torin down, he quickly climbed up to help Micheál down to the ground. Above them they heard the screech of the giant raven again. Looking up they saw the large black raven circling overheard, searching for its prey. Overcoming the pain in his stomach, with desperate fear, Micheál moved as best he could as he grabbed his brothers. With little time to spare, Micheál looked around and he saw what he needed. He shoved his brothers under a low fir tree. He then crawled in with them, and the three huddled in silent fear.

"It's the big black bird again!" Sneachta cried.

"Quiet." Alsandar whispered.

Dorcha laughed as her magic dark spell hit the sled and sent it splintering into pieces. At first she was angry when she found out Sneachta had survived. She had gone to look in her dark black pool under the tower to see how much Geal was suffering. But instead, she saw within the dark reflection Sneachta had not just survived but had a little human boy helping him. She would have to correct that. Dorcha wanted Geal to suffer. It had taken her days, but she finally caught up with Sneachta and his little friend. Dorcha was surprised to find the other two boys with them, but it didn't matter much to Dorcha. She would kill them all. It would serve the human children right for meddling in her affairs, and Sneachta would learn what it was like to face death again, but this time she would make sure all of them were dead before she left.

The party watched from under the fir tree, Micheál lamented, "Aw, Jeeze!" Alsandar looked at where Micheál was looking. There in the snow, the tracks clearly showed where they had gone to hide. Thinking quickly, Alsandar whipped out his wand and cast a cleaning spell on the snow. The ground shimmered, and the snow puffed up in a low wispy cloud and fell back down again as pristine as it had been before they landed or walked on it. Alsandar hoped he had covered their tracks in time and that the giant raven had not seen his magic. It wasn't long before they heard the beating of large wings coming closer. Soon it stopped, and the brothers could tell the large bird had perched not too far away. With their hearts pounding, they waited. Did Alsandar clean up their tracks in time? Would the large bird be able to find them? It was then Alsandar noticed the strong smell of dragon coming from Micheál. In all the fear and rush, he had forgotten it. The large bird would be able to smell them out. Quietly taking out his wand again, Alsandar used its magic to transfer the smell of the fir pine on to his brother. He hoped it was good enough to mask the scent.

Dorcha had watched as the splintered sled pieces and its occupants fell to the canopy below. She watched as they hit the trees and disappeared with in them. She waited longer to see what happened next, but there was nothing but silence. Dorcha circled overhead, trying to see through the treetops but could see nothing. Swooping down lower, she hunted for her prey. She would find what was left of them and make sure they too would disappear once and for all. This time she would be absolutely thorough! Dorcha landed on a tree branch, but to her surprise, she could see nothing, not even a track in the snow. It was as if Sneachta and his friends vanished as soon as they hit the trees. Dorcha was overcome with anxiety. *They had to be here!* she thought. If they got away and made it back to the snow queen, Dorcha would be finished. She had to find them and finish them quickly! As Dorcha pondered where to look, she caught the scent of dragon on the breeze. *They are hiding*, Dorcha thought. She sniffed the air again to pick up the trail, but the breeze changed, and all she could smell was the strong scent of pine and fir. She flitted to the ground and began looking under and behind everything.

Once again the brothers and Sneachta heard the flapping of the great wings as the raven descended to the ground. They knew the bird had landed and was looking for them. Reaching into his backpack, Alsandar took out a vial of strong sleeping potion and held it in ready. The giant raven was no fool. It began looking under the low-lying firs and pushing over boulders to see if there were any hiding places under them. The giant raven made its way closer to the brothers' hiding place. Then, as the brothers feared, they saw the great talons of the raven come to stand in front of their fir tree. The right talon of the raven reached to grab the lowest branches of their tree and pulled them up. Alsandar scooted forward, waiting for his chance. As the giant head peered under and looked at them, Alsandar threw the contents of the vial into the face of the raven. Its mouth had been open to screech at them, and most of the potion flew onto the raven's tongue. The raven squawked and screeched and staggered back. For a few moments, the raven just stood there. At first Alsandar thought the potion had not been strong enough, but then the great bird fell and hit the ground with a hard thump.

The brothers peaked out from under the fir tree. Sneachta had crawled up through the neck of Torin's coat, peered over his head, and held on to his ears for dear life as he too looked to see what had happened to the giant raven. It just laid there and didn't move. Cautiously the brothers crawled out from under the fir tree and crept closer to the fallen raven. When they had come close enough, to their surprise, they saw the raven had transformed some. The head had become that of a woman whose hair was comprised of both black feathers and long, black, silky hair. Her wings ended in hands with long talon like nails, and her lower legs had ended with normal ankles and feet. Her eyes were closed and oozing from her partly open mouth was the black liquid of sleeping potion pooling on the ground under her face. As Micheál watched her silently sleeping, he thought she looked beautiful in a dark sort of way. Her skin was pale of a bluish hue with her long, black, silky hair falling softly over her cheek. "Hey! That's Dorcha!" Alsandar cried. Micheál felt his heart stop. Micheál didn't think she was so beautiful any longer. He felt a great hatred swell up from within. Before anyone could think or stop him, Micheál had taken his sword from its sheath and raised it up high. In one quick swoosh, he brought it down and cut off her head. He then grabbed it by the feathery mixed hair and, running to gain momentum, threw it as far as he could. The rest stood in shock and awe at just how quickly it all had happened.

Sneachta watched the head fly beyond his line of sight. "Bye, bye," he said, feeling great relief at their sudden escape from the mean and evil raven.

Once it was over, Micheál fell to his knees and sobbed. All the hate, grief, and trauma he had been secretly carrying for all the years past surfaced and escaped from his soul. Great relief flowed over him as he realized it was finally finished. Dorcha was no more. It was done; it was over! Suddenly Micheál felt the pain in his stomach rear up again. He slumped over in the snow and held his stomach tightly, groaning in pain. Running over to him, Alsandar made him turn over. After opening up his coat, Alsandar lifted Micheál's sweater and shirt, and there they saw a very large bruise on his stomach. Thinking quickly, he reached in his backpack and took out an ointment his mother had made and smeared it over the large bruise. "I think he ruptured something when he hit the trees after the fall," Alsandar said. As the ointment sunk into his skin, Micheál instantly felt deep, penetrating warmth, which soothed the aching in his stomach. Looking up, Alsandar told Torin to find a shelter and gather some wood for a fire. They would not be able to travel further until Micheál had healed. "And, Torin, find a place far from that thing, would you?" Alsandar added as he pointed to the headless body of Dorcha. He knew the dead body would draw hungry animals, and they didn't want to be camped out close to that.

Farther up a hill, Torin had found the perfect spot. There was an old shallow cave under a rocky shelf in the woods over which he built a cover from pine limbs and other dead tree ruble he scavenged from the area. He helped Alsandar put together a stretcher made from pine limbs and a little magic from Alsandar's wand. Torin and Alsandar then dragged Micheál to the shelter inside and placed him on a soft bed of fir branches with a blanket from Micheál's pack. Using his magic wand again, Alsandar fortified the shelter with large rocks and small boulders, creating a warm safe haven. Satisfied everything was as good as they could make it, Alsandar went to Micheál's side. "Here, take this," Alsandar gently commanded as he held a vial up to Micheál's mouth.

"What is it?" he asked.

Alsandar smiled and replied, "Just a little something to help you sleep, Micheál. You know what Mom says—sleep heals better than anything else." Micheál drank it down and then grimaced.

"Ugh! Why does medicine have to taste so vile?"

Soon after, Micheál was sound asleep. Alsandar lifted his shirt again and drew magic symbols for healing on his brother's stomach and began the longest ritual of his life.

Chapter 9

Alsandar knew Micheál's injury was serious and could probably kill him, but there was nothing else to do, and they were too far away to get help in time, so he would have to depend on the medicine of his mother and his magic abilities to help his brother heal. For three days Micheál slept, and for three days Alsandar chanted and meditated nonstop on every healing spell he could remember, find in his encyclopedia, or create. Torin paced and built snow men and then in anger destroyed them and went back and forth sitting with his brothers and then out pacing again. Sneachta knew nothing of healing or injuries, so he sat quietly, keeping out of the way, and watched his friend suffer with anxiety over his oldest brother.

Sneachta didn't know what to do. He wished he was much larger so he could pet Torin on his back as Torin had pet him so many times when giving comfort to him. Instead Sneachta would just stroke Torin's ears and coo softly to him as his Aunt Geal had done for him many times in the past. Sneachta was fascinated with human ears. They were handy handles, small, and, in Sneachta's opinion, quite handsome things. Sneachta wished he had small ears like Torin. But what little Sneachta could do still didn't calm Torin's anxiety over his brother Micheál.

Alsandar had not told Torin how seriously Micheál was injured, but he could guess from the time Alsandar was taking with his magic it had to be pretty bad. Torin didn't really know what a rupture was or how bad it could be. He wished he knew magic so he could help. He also wished he had his mother's knowledge of healing to help in that way as well. He made a promise to himself that when they got home, he would pay close attention to his mother's skills and ask Alsandar to teach him magic. At the end of the third day, Alsandar was completely spent. He knew he could do no more, and the rest would be up to Micheál. Alsandar collapsed back against the cave wall and fell into a deep sleep. Torin spent the next two days eating, petting Sneachta, sleeping, and watching his brothers sleep.

Torin was lying in his warm bed at home. He smelled his mother's cooking and knew soon he would have to get up for breakfast. As he lay snuggled comfortably under his warm covers, he heard his bedroom door open and soft footsteps come close to his bed. Suddenly he felt hands upon his shoulders shaking him. He then heard a loud familiar voice yell at him, "Torin, Torin wake up!" Startled, Torin woke up.

"What? I was sleeping," Torin grumbled, thinking he was at home again. Torin opened his eyes and looked around him. He wasn't back home in his own bed after all. He was in a small cave. Once his vision had cleared, Torin looked around and saw Alsandar still sleeping against the wall and Micheál sitting up next to him. Torin sat up and looked at the person whose voice had shaken him from his dream.

"Micheál, you're okay!" Torin said, giving his brother a big hug. Hearing Torin, Sneachta ran back inside the cave. He had gone out to sit in the early morning sun and watch it sparkle on the snow-covered ground and hope that everything would work out after all. Upon seeing Micheál sitting up and awake, Sneachta ran up his torso and crawled on his head.

Peering down over his forehead to look him in the eye, Sneachta said, "You awake now? Feeling better I hope."

Micheál laughed and gently grabbed Sneachta from his head and cuddled him in his arms. Gently stroking his back, Micheál said, "Yeah, I'm better now. But I'm starving!"

In a state of excitement, both Sneachta and Torin jumped for Torin's backpack to get some venison and bread. Sneachta crashed into Torin's hand and went flying. When Torin looked to see if Sneachta was all right, he saw that Sneachta was actually still flying. Torin watched for a few seconds, waiting to see where he would land. But Sneachta didn't. He watched in surprise as Sneachta flew around in circles, a bit unsteady, yet he kept up his short flight until he grew tired. His landing was clumsy, but Sneachta didn't care. It was his first flight. He was excited. Instinctually Sneachta had opened his wings as Torin's hand knocked him in the air. It wasn't until a second went by that Sneachta realized he was flying. "Sneachta, you flew!" Torin exclaimed.

"Yes! I flew," Sneachta replied, very excited.

"Do it again! Toss me in the air."

Torin hesitated. He didn't want to hurt Sneachta again. He decided to wait. "Let's eat first, Sneachta. Micheál is hungry," Torin said. Slightly disappointed, Sneachta agreed.

Torin went outside of the shelter entrance and quickly had the small campfire going with the magic fire light. He could hear Micheál in the cave trying to wake up Alsandar. "Wake up, Alsandar, its breakfast time," Micheál said. Alsandar stirred, mumbled a slight threat at his brother for disturbing him, and rolled over on his side and continued to sleep.

Torin poked his head back into the shelter and said, "Let him sleep, Micheál. He was up for three straight days healing you."

"Three days?" Micheál asked.

Torin shook his head yes. "I guess you were badly hurt from the fall. We were so worried about you," Torin replied. Turning back, Torin started to cook the meat over the fire after he gave Sneachta a piece of raw venison.

Alsandar had slept through the day and the night. Micheál was still weak, and he too snoozed off and on. Torin spent most of the time outside tossing Sneachta into the air while he perfected his flight abilities and grew strong enough for longer periods of flight. As Torin watched Sneachta happily flying around, he noticed that Sneachta was becoming quite larger. It would not be long before Sneachta could no longer fit inside his coat. On the last toss, Torin felt something sticking to his hands. As he looked at them he saw it was the skin from Sneachta's body. Sneachta's skin was starting to come off. Torin was startled. He hadn't realized he was hurting Sneachta. "Sneachta, I don't think I should toss you any more. It's rubbing off your skin!" Torin told Sneachta, feeling alarmed. They had just got through one bad incident with Micheál, and Torin didn't want to go through another with Sneachta's losing his skin. Surprised, Sneachta looked and scratched at the areas he was shedding. It didn't hurt any; in fact it felt quite good to scratch off the lose skin. "Sneachta, don't do that. You'll take your skin off!" Torin said as he watched the little dragon scratching himself. Sneachta ignored him and continued to scratch. Torin was worried something was very wrong with Sneachta.

As Torin ran toward the little dragon scratching himself in the snow, he saw a huge patch of skin suddenly come off. In fact all the skin on Sneachta became lose, and to Torin's surprise, the skin over his entire body gave way and became a loose shell. Sneachta licked it off, and under the old skin, Sneachta had soft smooth scales unlike the lizard skin he had had before that gleamed and sparkled in the winter sun. Torin sat down beside his little friend, relieved as he realized Sneachta was just shedding. Picking Sneachta up, Torin noticed Sneachta had grown far much larger than he had realized since they had left home. "You grew Sneachta," Torin said.

"Feels good to have old skin off," Sneachta commented. Torin examined his new skin in the light. His scales looked like dragon scales now, and the small white shingles sparkled with many different colors in the sun, just like the snow reflecting the sunlight.

Chapter 10

Finally Alsandar woke up, and Micheál felt strong enough to continue on their journey. Alsandar was disappointed he had slept through all the changes. He felt a deep satisfaction that his magic had worked on his brother, helped no doubt by his mother's herbal ointment. He was becoming a stronger sorcerer. It was a good day for Alsandar. Micheál was well again, and Sneachta was finally able to fly on his own. He knew Sneachta would grow fast now that he had lost his baby dragon skin, and it would be easier for the brothers not having to carry a growing dragon so much. Sneachta would also be able to navigate better since he could fly high up into the air and follow his path back home. And best of all, Dorcha was dead! That was the best change of all. She would trouble them no more. Micheál was his hero, and when the valley people found out, no doubt he would be a great hero to them as well. Alsandar doubted he would have had the courage his older brother did to just up and chop off her head like that, but it had to be done. Dorcha would have been furious when she woke up, and there was no telling what kind of evil revenge she would have unleashed upon them.

As the brothers walked past the place where Micheál had killed Dorcha, they saw her body had been eaten on by wild animals. The snow was completely melted all around her half-eaten carcass, and the ground was black with even blacker thorny brambles growing in and out of the openings of her bones and torn flesh. Alsandar knew that this would be an evil spot from now on. When a faerie died, the earth demands an exchange, and the thorny brambles were hers. A faeries body and soul were made from the natural elements of the earth and so upon destruction of that life, all were returned to the earth. Forever more her spirit would be entombed in this place and the thorny brambles served as a warning to anyone not to come near it. The brothers and Sneachta gave it a wide berth. They would have to warn everyone about this spot. Eventually the brambles would grow large enough to ensnare anything that came within its reach. Alsandar wondered what kind of flowers the bramble would produce in the spring. They would be black, no doubt.

The travelers had walked and fallen and stumbled in deep snow for quite some time while Alsandar tried to think of another way for them to travel. They agreed it wasn't wise to make another flying device since they could be easily attacked from the air. While they didn't have to worry about Dorcha anymore, there were still other things like wyverns and wild dragons who had ventured out for a snack. "Let's make another sled," Torin suggested.

"Yeah, a magic one," Micheál agreed. Alsandar thought about it. He would have to look in his encyclopedia of magic to find a spell that would make the sled move on its own when they didn't have a hill to go down. It was easier to make large things fly in the air than to move them on the ground. When they stopped for lunch, Alsandar went through his encyclopedia, and Torin, Sneachta, and Micheál looked for wood to construct another sled from. Suddenly Torin had an idea.

"I know. Let's make a raft with a sail!" Torin said.

"A raft with a sail?" Micheál questioned.

"Yes, a raft with a sail. It will come in handy if we have to cross any water as well," Torin explained.

After a minute of thinking about Torin's idea, Micheál thought it would be better than a sled. "You can be pretty cleaver sometimes, little brother." Micheál laughed as he playfully smacked Torin on the head.

The brothers turned to Alsandar with Torin's idea which made Alsandar very pleased. They each had a couple of blankets for the sail, and with a sail it would be easier to move the raft, much easier than it would a plain sled. The raft would be like a sled with sails. Its flat bottom would easily go over the deep snow. Instead of trying to enchant the raft, Alsandar would use his wand to create a magic breeze for the sail to propel them in any direction they wished to go. After lunch the brothers gathered the wood they needed and built the raft. Soon they were on their way, traveling fast as Sneachta occasionally flew up above the trees giving them directions. The boys were delighted as they sailed happily over the snow through the forest. It wasn't every day a boy could go rafting through the woods. Even with all the hardships they had encountered, the journey was turning out to be quite fun as well. Between Alsandar's magic, Torin's cleaver ideas, and Micheál's courage and strength, they had come a long way.

Micheál was enchanted with Sneachta. Since Dorcha's death he started to feel good about dragons again and getting to know Sneachta had changed his mind about them completely. Some dragons were good, and some dragons were bad—that's just the way it was. Micheál thought that when he returned home, he might just take up his studies to be a dragoneer again.

As the sun sank low in the western sky, the brothers and Sneachta made camp for the night. They parked the raft under a low pine tree next to a rocky croft and built a shelter around it in case another blizzard hit during the night. They used the magic fire light for warmth and cooking so they wouldn't burn the raft. Alsandar drew a magic protection circle around the croft to keep anything wild away, and Micheál suggested that Sneachta do his duty as much as he could around the encampment. The smell of dragon would make any wild creature think twice about coming anywhere near them while they slept.

During the night there was something the smell of dragon drew to the encampment, something Micheál hadn't thought of. Several dark figures sat perched on nearby tree limbs watching the strange structure under the pine tree next to the croft that had the smell of dragon around it. They didn't like the smell; it meant to them a dragon had moved into their territory. During the cold season, it meant food would be scarcer with that kind of competition. It was unexpected since dragons slept in hibernation most of the winter except to come out occasionally when extremely hungry. Their simple minds didn't wonder why a dragon had suddenly moved in when winter was well on its way. They just knew one was suddenly here in their territory. The wind picked up while the silent figures kept watch. Soon it began to blow hard, and snowflakes whipped around them in the air, signaling another winter storm was about to blow through. The figures spread their large wings and flew off into the dark night back to their warren to wait out the storm.

Chapter 11

When the brothers and Sneachta woke the next morning, they could not open the entrance of their shelter. The blizzard during the night had buried them. But this did not worry the brothers. Only Sneachta was apprehensive about how they might get out. Alsandar told Sneachta that he would get them out, but first they had to eat. Using the magic fire light to cook with, the brothers had their breakfast. Once done, Alsandar took his wand, raised it in the air, and shouted, "Pléasc Oscailte!"(Blast Open!) A large white ball of energy flew from the tip of his wand and exploded within the shelter. Alsandar had used too much magic. In such a small space, the blast left everyone disheveled with the smell of burnt hair and cloth permeating the air. Coughing in the small smoke-filled enclosure, the brothers looked at each other's blackened faces and whipped frumpled hair. Instead of getting upset, they all laughed. They looked too funny to get angry. No one was seriously hurt, but the blast left all their ears ringing.

"Next time, Alsandar, we'll try something different, like digging out the old-fashioned way!" Micheál said as he combed down his hair. Alsandar picked up his sorcerer's cap and noticed a small burn hole through the top of it.

"Rats!" Alsandar murmured as he wiggled his finger through the hole. He wished his mother was there. She could fix the hole in no time at all.

After an hour of digging out, re-rigging, and repairing the raft, the four were on their way again. The sun shone on the sparkly snow, and the fresh cold air whipped through the sails of the raft. It was a happy morning for the travelers. Micheál spent his time drawing pictures of Sneachta and telling jokes. Alsandar taught Torin small basic spells while he kept the raft going with his magic wand. "Why do brownies never invite pixies for tea?" Micheál asked. Alsandar and Torin looked at each other. They didn't know the answer.

Sneachta, who had just flown into rest, answered, "Because they leave the place dusty when they leave." The brothers laughed.

"How did you know, Sneachta?" Micheál asked.

"Because I hear a lot of gossip about them. It's true, you know. They leave pixie dust everywhere they go," Sneachta answered. "House brownies don't like them. Pixies are difficult creatures anyway, so no one really has much to do with them unless they have to," Sneachta explained further. While Sneachta told the brothers what he knew of brownies and pixies, the raft sailed through a small canyon.

Suddenly the four heard a blood-chilling cry echoing all around them. Startled, they looked to find the source, but all they could see was the canyon walls and forest trees. They could see nothing of what was making the sound. As the sound came closer, Sneachta's sharp ears found the source of the cries. "Up there!" cried Sneachta as he pointed to the sky behind them. The brothers looked up and saw three wyverns heading straight for them. In a panic Alsandar intensified the magic wind in the sails, hoping they could out run them. Torin grabbed Alsandar's bow and arrows while Micheál drew his sword in anticipation of a battle with the wyverns. Faster and faster, Alsandar made the raft sail until it was almost impossible to control. Sooner or later they would crash and have to fight, or the wyverns would catch up with them. Either way it was getting very difficult for Alsandar to hold his magic at such intensity. Torin drew an arrow and let it fly. To his surprise the arrow flew straight on course and pierced the closest wyvern through the head. It dropped, instantly crashing on the snowy ground. Torin had not practiced much with a bow and arrow.

"Shoot, Torin!" Alsandar yelled! "Shoot and concentrate on the wyvern you're aiming at!" Torin did as his brother said, and he shot another one down. Upon seeing its two companions already killed, the third wyvern turned back and left the travelers alone.

Alsandar relaxed on his wind spell, and the raft slowly came to a stop. The brothers and Sneachta cheered Torin and ruffled him up a bit in congratulations. "You did it, Torin. You saved us!" Micheál exclaimed with great cheer.

"Those were magic arrows, Torin," Alsandar explained. "It takes someone with magic talent to use them. They don't work for just anyone." Torin was surprised. He was still so young and didn't know what kind of talent he might have yet. Though he had watched Alsandar in the past practice his magic, he had never exhibited any magic as far as he could remember. "I wondered about you," Alsandar said. "When you told us about how you made the flame from the magic fire light jump to the saber tooth, I knew you had some magic in you, but now I know you have a lot. Only a person with real magic can do what you did." Torin was very pleased. Up until then it had always been his big brothers doing marvelous things, and now he had done something marvelous as well. After the shock and relief of their near catastrophe wore off, the four continued on their journey.

The next three days were uneventful. The brothers and Sneachta were enjoying their trip together and spent a lot of time playing in the snow, laughing and telling stories. Alsandar took some extra time to show Torin new magic spells, and Micheál trained him in swordplay with sticks Alsandar had made into wooden swords. Sneachta had grown rapidly since shedding his baby skin and was now too large to hide in Torin's coat anymore. As each day passed, Sneachta became more excited as he knew he was getting closer to home. He thought maybe he should just say goodbye and make it on his own now that he could fly, but the comfort of having others to help him and the past experiences of how dangerous the wild can be put him off from such a decision. But most of all, what kept Sneachta from flying home on his own was that he had grown to love the brothers and didn't want to part with them. The brothers had become part of his life, and the journey they had shared with him bonded each of them together in a way that never is easy to break.

"Are we getting any closer, Sneachta?" Torin asked as the wind-whipped snow flurries stung his face. They had not found shelter quickly enough, for the winter storm was now engulfing the shelter they were trying to throw together.

"We are close, I think," Sneachta answered as he tried to help, blowing his small flames to melt any snow piles that got in their way. Finally after what seemed an eternity of struggling in the cold wind and snow, the shelter was finished. The brothers shivered as they hurried to get under cover.

"So where is it exactly you live, Sneachta?" Micheál asked as the four quickly sat around the magic fire light to get warm and dry.

"I live with Geal," Sneachta answered.

"Who's Geal?" Alsandar asked.

"My aunt," Sneachta replied "She took care of me after my mother died." Though Sneachta had told them what had happened to him, he had not thought to tell them from where and whom he came from. There had been too many events and too much fun in between for Sneachta to think of its importance. Micheál thought a bit about Sneachta's answer. Sneachta was a white dragon, and the only other white dragon he knew of belonged to the winter queen. Though it was rare, white dragons had been known to be born from other colors of dragons but only if there had been white dragons in their linage.

"Do you know what kind of dragon your mother was?" Micheál asked.

Sneachta replied, "She was a great big dragon." Sneachta didn't know much about other dragons yet. All he knew was what his Aunt Geal had told him about his mother.

"Was she white like you?" Micheál asked.

"Why, yes, she was," Sneachta answered. Micheál was getting a funny feeling in his stomach. The only known white dragon of his life time was the winter queen's. Micheál searched through his memory for the snow faerie's actual name. Then he hit upon it; it was Geal Geamhradh. The name Geal had to be Geal Geamhradh, the Winter Queen. In fact he was sure of it. The name Geal had never been heard of before in human circles. It was a very strange name to begin with. Alsandar looked at his older brother. He, too, knew something was funny about the white dragon's answers.

"Do you know what your mother's name was?" Alsandar asked.

"Bain," Sneachta replied. Alsandar closed his eyes. Sneachta was the winter queen's dragon! Alsandar remembered Bain. She was a sight no one would soon forget! He was so scared and enthralled at the same time the first time he had seen her with the winter queen. She was badly wounded though. But Bain still stood proud and tall even with her deeply cut bloodied wounds across her great powerful body. She still amazed Alsandar to this day. She was a beautiful sight in the eyes of the small apprentice sorcerer so many years ago. It broke Alsandar's heart to hear of her death.

Taking a large piece of venison out of Torin's pack (which had grown much lighter now that Sneachta had a bigger appetite), Micheál tossed it over to Sneachta who caught it in his mouth and gulped it down. After Sneachta had swallowed his meal, Micheál asked Sneachta to tell them about his Aunt Geal. "She is very beautiful and sparkly most the time," Sneachta answered. He went on to tell them that his Aunt Geal lived in a big ice castle on the snow-covered cliffs above a huge frozen loch high on a mountain top. The snow never melted where his Aunt Geal lived. She was always kind and loved to talk with the animals who lived in the forest below the frozen loch. She rarely had visitors, and when she became lonely, she went to the forest to see her friends.

"What happened to your mother—why did she die?" Torin asked, feeling sorry for Sneachta. Sneachta looked down at the ground and picked at the wood on the raft he was sitting on.

"There was a great battle between my mother and Dorcha's great black dragon, Droch. She was hurt too bad to get well again. The black dragon was a dragon of darkness, and his poison went to deep into her wounds," Sneachta answered. Sneachta turned and looked at Micheál. "I'm glad Dorcha is dead!" Sneachta exclaimed. Micheál felt relief. He was glad he had killed Dorcha as well, but at the same time he felt grieved at taking the life of another. He knew it had been necessary. Dorcha would have killed them all for sure. Sneachta fiddled with his tail as he thought of his mother. "It's okay. Actually, I never knew my mother. The only mother I have now is Aunt Geal, and she is the best mother a dragon can have." Sneachta's heart began to break again. He missed her terribly and wanted to get home as soon as possible. He knew she would be very worried about him.

The brothers sat in silence. Micheál and Alsandar grew worried. They knew now the little white dragon belonged to the snow faerie Geal Geamhradh, the powerful winter queen. That was why Dorcha had come after them. The vision in the attic before Micheál and Alsandar left to find Torin suddenly became clear to Alsandar. Sneachta, Dorcha, and Droch were all tied together. Geal Geamhradh had killed Droch, and Dorcha had, in return, kidnapped and then tried to kill Sneachta in revenge. But because Torin had found Sneachta, they all became entangled Dorcha's mess. Dorcha had failed luckily. Alsandar wondered if it was fate behind it all. Though a lot of bad things had happened to them since that day Torin had found the little dragon, many other things had finally come full circle. A great deal of healing had taken place, and new understandings unfolded between Alsandar and his brothers. Alsandar wondered what would happen next. The four sat in silence, staring at the magic fire light. The wind howled outside and occasionally rattled the shelter.

Chapter 12

Micheál shivered a little as he thought of the situation the brothers now found themselves in. The storm outside didn't make it any easier for Micheál to think about. He felt the storm was just part of the events he knew would soon be unfolding for them. Micheál knew they would have to enter into the realm of the faeries in order to return Sneachta home. It was a dangerous thing for a human to do. Faeries rarely let anyone return once they found their secret places. No one knew the great white dragon had died. They didn't know how fateful the battle between the great white dragon and the great black dragon had been. No one knew how costly the sacrifice Sneachta's mother made had actually been. Surely Bain had known how deadly the poison of a great black dragon was, but she did it anyway. Micheál's heart swelled with great respect for Bain and her incredible bravery. He wished he had gotten to know her. Micheál reached for Sneachta and held him in his arms. Sneachta didn't understand the sudden affection from Micheál but relished it anyway. Sneachta settled quietly in Micheál's lap while they continued to watch the glow and enjoy the warmth of the magic fire light. Both the winter queen and Bain had paid dearly for saving the people of the Valley of the Dragon. Breaking the silence, Micheál turned to his brother Alsandar and said, "What do we do? On one hand, Bain and Geal

Geamhradh gave up a lot to save our people. On the other hand, we shouldn't go any further."

Alsandar thought about it for a moment. He looked at his brothers and then at little Sneachta. He was amazed. Before him sat a great white dragon that would grow up to be the most powerful dragon in the land. He had never been this close to such an amazing creature. Alsandar looked at Sneachta and replied, "True, but now we can do something for them, something for Bain, the greatest dragon ever to have lived!" Micheál looked at his water flask. Alsandar grinned as if he read his mind. Smiling at each other Alsandar and Micheál took up their water flasks and held them high. "To Bain!" they shouted and then drank their water.

Torin knew something was wrong by the way his older brothers seemed to be talking in circles and the worried look on their faces. To Torin it was simple—return Sneachta home and then they too return home. But then he remembered Micheál's saying, "On the other hand we shouldn't go any further."

"What's wrong?" Torin asked. "I know something is wrong. You don't seem too excited about getting Sneachta home anymore."

Micheál looked down at Sneachta who was settled comfortably in his lap. Stroking his back between his wings, Micheál hugged the little dragon. "I love you Sneachta." he said.

Sneachta was surprised and touched at the same time. Micheál loved him! Sneachta turned and hugged Micheál back. "I love you too, my friend."

"You see, Torin," Alsandar replied, "Sneachta belongs to the winter queen. And in order to return Sneachta home, we have to enter into the realm of the faeries."

"And that can be dangerous," Micheál added. Torin didn't understand. He didn't know much about faeries except that some were bad and some were good, and it was best to just leave them alone if you could. It was like the bees in the clover fields; they do good things, like make honey and pollinate the flowers, but you don't mess with them, or you get stung.

"Do Faeries sting?" Torin asked. The older brothers laughed. "Some do," Micheál replied.

It took Sneachta a few moments to understand what the brothers were saying. He now realized how different his Aunt Geal, a faerie, was from the humans. Up until now they just both existed in the same world side by side. His Aunt Geal had never explained the concept of difference. "What is so bad about entering the realm of the faeries?" Sneachta asked.

Micheál explained. "They don't like it when humans discover where they live, Sneachta, and they don't let them return home again."

Sneachta was horrified. He could not imagine his Aunt Geal would be so mean as to not let the brothers return home. He thought about Torin's question. Sneachta had never seen her sting anything. He wondered who made that rule and why faeries were so protective over their realms. "Why is that?" Sneachta asked.

"I'm not sure, but I think it is because, like faeries and dragons, there can be bad humans, and they are just protecting themselves," Alsandar answered.

"I see; there is good and bad in all things," Sneachta sadly answered.

The matter of the final leg of the journey would take time to decide on. Entering the realm of the faeries would not be easy, and they had no idea where or how to enter at. Both worlds exist upon each other, but only faeries could easily cross between the two unless a human was clever enough and brave enough to figure out how. Although, there were certain times on certain days of the year the two worlds melded together. On these certain days, it was three days before and three days after a solstice. Occasionally during these days an unsuspecting traveler became caught in the faerie realm and could never return home again. The brothers talked about all the possible answers and had decided upon at least one thing. Geal Geamhradh had sacrificed a lot to save their people, and because of her they were alive today. It was the least they could do to sacrifice their lives in order to return Sneachta, especially after Bain had died for the cause. What they could not figure out was how to get word to their family and explain why it was they might never come back again. They hoped the winter queen would at least be merciful enough to grant them the request to get word to their family and let them know what had happened.

Sneachta was beside himself with anguish. The brothers had gone through so much to help him return home. He was certain his Aunt Geal would be kind to them. But he did understand why she might not let them return home again. He would have to figure something out. Sneachta promised the brothers that when he grew large enough, he would return them home, even against the winter queen's wishes. But Micheál explained that would just cause more trouble. Dorcha's wrath had been bad enough, but to have such anger turned on his family and Sneachta by a powerful faerie like Geal Geamhradh for betrayal would be much, much worse. They decided they would take what came, and that would be the right thing and the most honorable thing to do. Sneachta was overcome by the loyalty of his friends and how they would give up so much for him and his aunt. However, since Sneachta's loyalty and love was just as strong for them, he could not let it happen. When the time was right, Sneachta decided he would quietly sneak away and find the rest of his way alone. He could fly now, and the rest of the journey by flight would be much quicker than on the ground, for he could fly much faster than the raft.

Chapter 13

After waiting out the winter storm, the brothers and Sneachta set out again. By midday Sneachta flew high in the air again to navigate and saw the forest he had started from in the near distance. They were getting close now. It was time for him to make his break. After they had stopped for lunch, Sneachta wandered off with the excuse he had to relieve himself again. When he was far enough away, he flew into the sky. His heart grew heavy for betraying his friends like that and not being able to say a proper goodbye. He hoped that some day they would forgive him. The brothers waited and waited for Sneachta to return, but he never came back. They worried something had happened to him. They searched and searched but found no sign of him.

The brothers could not rest until they knew they had done all they could to find Sneachta. After rafting through the area and finding no sign of Sneachta, Alsandar used his spell for finding lost items, but it didn't work. Sneachta wasn't an item; he was a living creature. So he decided to use the spell of insight. They didn't have anything that belonged to Sneachta, though, so Alsandar wasn't sure if it would work very well. Sneachta had spent a great deal of time on the raft with them, so Alsandar used the raft. He hoped it had enough of Sneachta's energy imprinted on it. Once he had performed all the pre-rituals for protection, Alsandar cast his spell.

The brothers watched as a smoky form slowly billowed into a scene in the center of the raft. There they saw a sky view of the area they were in as if the vision of insight were flying over them above. The vision flew over the woods and then over a great frozen loch. As the brothers looked at the loch, the vision suddenly seemed to explode. Dagger-like shards of ice shot out from the vision toward them. Instinctively the brothers ducked and hit the ground. To their surprise they were not hurt. The shards were just a vision and not real. "What was that?" Micheál exclaimed.

Picking themselves up off the ground and dusting off the snow, the brothers looked at each other. "What does that mean?" Torin asked.

"What does what mean?"Alsandar repeated, confused and shaken by what they had just seen.

"The shards of ice exploding in our faces!" Micheál yelled back.

Alsandar thought for a moment and then answered, "I think it is either a warning, or the vision tried to enter the realm of the faeries, or something attacked Sneachta.

"So what do we do now?" Torin asked. Torin's heart was breaking over the loss of Sneachta. He couldn't understand how Sneachta would just leave like that. "You don't suppose Sneachta took off on his own, do you?" Torin asked.

"Why do you say that?" Alsandar asked.

"Because he seemed a little upset when he heard we might not be able to return home again if we entered the winter queen's realm," Torin answered as his eyes filled with tears.

Micheál grabbed Torin and held him close. He understood Torin's sorrow. "It kind of looks that way, Torin. I think Sneachta has gone home on his own," Micheál said.

Micheál knew Torin was probably right. Sneachta did seem a bit concerned at the time that the brothers would not be able to return home, but he had said nothing about them splitting up. "I think that is what he did," Torin said, feeling sad he never got to say goodbye.

"Well, we better be sure first," Micheál said. "It could be possible something got him, and I'll never forgive myself if I don't at least try to find out if he is okay or not."

Alsandar agreed, "We'll go as far as the loch, and if we find nothing, then it is probably a sure bet Sneachta found his way home again." Alsandar also worried about the possibility that something could have gotten Sneachta. Maybe that was what the exploding shards of ice meant, something had gotten to Sneachta, and somehow the ice in the loch could have meant he crashed into it. Like his brothers, Alsandar felt they needed to find out for sure just in case.

Torin felt happy again. If Sneachta did take off on his own, at least now he might get the chance to say a proper farewell to his friend. On the other hand, his brother's worries crept into his mind, and he soon found himself anxious to find Sneachta and make sure he was okay.

By late afternoon, right before sunset, the brothers had found the loch. The air was incredibly cold, much colder than they had ever felt it before. The frozen loch had a strange translucent mist covering its surface that rose from the ground. The sun didn't shine through a murky sky even though it was near sundown, and no light or colors showed where a setting sun might shine, even through the clouds. As the brothers looked around, they saw lights flicker and bounce from various objects, like trees and boulders, reflecting off the mist that covered the loch. Whatever noises the brothers made seemed to echo as if the loch were in a canyon, yet they were not in a canyon. It would be dark soon, and the brothers had to find a place to shelter again. While the brothers looked around for shelter, they felt an eerie presence of something they could not see. It made them feel uneasy, as if they were not welcome, but still they looked for shelter. After a bit of time, they noticed the cold became more intense and went right through their thick clothing. It felt as if they were slowly freezing to death. The magic fire light helped some, but it was not enough.

As they walked to look for a place to shelter, their feet grew heavy. When they looked down on their boots, they saw ice was forming on their feet and slowly working up toward their legs. It was becoming very difficult for them to move any more. "Oh no!" Alsandar cried.

"What's happening?" Torin yelled.

"We found the realm of the snow faerie," Micheál said. Holding out his arms to his brothers, he calmly said, "Come here." As the brothers went into each other's arms, Micheál said, "I love you," and held them as close as he could. Micheál knew there was nothing they could do. The snow faerie's protective realm was far more powerful than the three of them were, and now they would be frozen forever in each other's arms. If they were to die, at least they would die together.

As Micheál wondered how it had been so easy to just walk into the realm of the winter queen Alsandar asked, "What day is it?" Then it dawned on Micheál. It was the day before the eve of the winter solstice, one of the first days the world of faeries and humans began to merge.

Before the ice encasement made its way to their waists, the brothers had already fallen asleep from the cold. As Torin fell into his deep sleep, his last thoughts were of his mother the night he gave her his last hug. *I'm sorry, Mom. I love you!* Torin thought as he passed from consciousness. There the brothers stood like frozen statues in each other's arms.

Chapter 14

Geal Geamhradh sat on her ice throne, melancholy for days. She had searched and searched and found no sign of Sneachta. The large black bird had probably eaten Sneachta, and her heart was utterly broken. When she could take the grief no more, she bent over the arm of her throne and sobbed heavily. It felt like her life was over, but for a faerie like her, she knew she would not die easily but rather waste away in sorrow for centuries to come. The snow would never fall again in her land once she finally died and her heart was too broken to care. "I'm so sorry," Geal sobbed over and over again.

Suddenly she felt a cool hand on her arm. As she looked she saw the small white talons of a small white dragon. Looking up with her tear-stained face, there she saw her little lost dragon, Sneachta. He had grown quite a bit and had his dragon scales now, but the queen knew in an instant it was Sneachta. "Sneachta!" cried out the winter queen in surprise. She grabbed him up in her arms, sobbing her apologies over and over for not protecting him.

"It's okay. I had help," Sneachta gleefully replied as he hugged his Aunt Geal back just as hard. "I missed you so much!" he said.

Sneachta explained what had happened to him and how Dorcha had taken him and how his friend Micheál had killed her. Sneachta told the winter queen all about their long, hard, and sometimes fun journey. Geal Geamhradh's heart filled with immense gratitude. She wanted to find the brothers and thank them for the safe return of her snow dragon. Sneachta's heart filled with joy. He would be able to say a proper goodbye after all. The winter queen called the wind to her side, and off the two went in search of the brothers. They had no sooner crossed the frozen loch when Sneachta looked down and saw the frozen raft he had spent so much time on with the brothers. The winter queen's heart sank. She knew what time of year it was and that the two realms had opened up to each other. She also knew what happened when the uninvited crossed into her realm. She rushed down and found the brothers embraced together. The ice had almost encased their entire bodies. Sneachta cried out in horror. He could not believe that after all they had been through and that even after leaving them to save them they would die.

The winter queen went to the frozen bodies of the frozen brothers and took them in her arms. "Come, Sneachta, it will be okay," Geal calmly said. "They are mine now, and I will do what I can to help them." Sneachta's hopes rose. Once the winter queen had the brother's back at the palace, she set them in a magic circle which thawed them out. Slowly the ice vanished while Sneachta paced back and forth anxiously waiting. Once all the ice was gone, the brothers woke up again. As they regained their senses, they looked around and found themselves in a great and beautiful throne room made of ice. To their surprise the brothers also found they were not cold anymore.

"Hallo," said a voice from above them. Looking up they saw the snow faerie looking down on them from her throne. Sneachta, who had finally stopped pacing, jumped down from his place next to Geal, squealing with delight, and ran toward the brothers. The brothers stood in awe looking at the winter queen. Geal Geamhradh was just as beautiful as Sneachta had described her. Her pale blue skin sparkled like the sun shining on a smooth snowy surface, and her long white hair glistened with many colors of reflected light, like the sun shining down on a ground of virgin snow. She wore white silks and had the most beautiful grand wings the brothers could ever imagine. Her crown was made from sparkling ice crystals and gave off a glowing light that mesmerized the brothers. The brothers knelt down before her.

The winter queen smiled. "I owe you so much for the safe return of Sneachta. I will grant you any wish I can that you desire."

"We wish to go home!" the brothers answered in unison.

The winter queen sighed. "Well, about that there is a problem. You entered my realm, and now you belong to me. You must become immortal and dwell with the faeries. There is nothing I can do about that. It is the law of the faeries, and I cannot break that law."

Torin began to cry. The thought of never seeing his parents again broke his heart. Micheál and Alsandar hugged him and then each other. "We knew the price we would have to pay when we found out who Sneachta was," Micheál said.

"We decided anyway to return Sneachta for you, Alsandar said.

The winter queen was surprised. "For me, but why?" she asked.

"In gratitude of the great sacrifice you and Bain paid for saving the people of the Valley of the Dragon," Micheál answered.

The Queen was astonished. "Are you from the Valley of the Dragon?" she asked. Alsandar and Micheál told the Queen about their family, where they lived, and what the people of the valley had been through since her last known visit. Her heart filled with compassion and gratitude for the brothers. After all they had done for her and Sneachta; she would have to find a way around the law of the faeries.

While Geal sat thinking, a thought occurred to her. Dorcha was dead. What would become of her realm? With Dorcha gone, her realm would disappear, or, worse, another dark faerie would claim her tower and take her place. Geal could not let that happen. Suddenly, Geal had a brilliant idea. She would claim Dorcha's realm and have the brothers be her caretakers. In that way they could return home to the Valley of the Dragon and still belong to her. As she quickly explained her plan, she called the wind to her once more. They would all have to ride the wind. Without a full-grown dragon, she could not carry them. Her wings were powerful but not strong enough for all three brothers and Sneachta. The wind would carry them faster than a dragon could, anyway. Even Geal herself could not fly as fast as the wind. Time was of the essence. They had to get to Dorcha's tower before news of her death got out. With her magic protecting the brothers from the freezing cold of her wind, they rushed off into the sky toward the Valley of the Dragon.

When the wind travelers had reached Dorcha's tower, it was no longer black but grey as the original stones had been. The dark fog that had forever encased her realm was gone, and the snow-covered land looked like the rest of the valley except it too had an eerie surreal ambiance. Dorcha's dark magic around her tower was now gone, but the brothers could still tell it belonged to the realm of the faeries. The travelers walked upon the balcony Dorcha herself had spent so much time watching Droch destroy the valley below. The place had a peaceful stillness about it. It was as if a great cleansing had swept through Dorcha's domain. The only sound they heard was the sound of their own footsteps upon the stone floor. Geal paused and reached out with her mind to catch any signs of other faeries in and around the tower. She sensed no one but the brothers and Sneachta. They had arrived in time. Stepping back, Geal cast a powerful spell claiming the realm of Dorcha.

When the five walked into Dorcha's tower, they saw it was elegantly decorated with fine furniture and rich tapestries. As Torin stood in front of a tapestry to examine its picture, he gasped. Alarmed, Micheál and Alsandar ran to see what had surprised Torin. They knew Dorcha's evil and the pieces of her darkness could still be hiding in the tower. Torin's brothers feared for Torin's safety. Looking up at the tapestry where Torin was staring, they were stunned. As they gazed at the tapestry, they saw a horrific scene of unimaginable nightmares of war and chaos. Geal walked up behind the three and looked while Sneachta whimpered and hid behind Torin. "Well, that kind of stuff will simply have to go!" Geal exclaimed. Torin and the rest stared at the tapestry for a long time. It was perfect despite its diabolical scene. The tapestry looked as real as if they were looking through a window. "Go find a dustpan and broom, Sneachta," Geal ordered. Sneachta hesitated. He didn't want to go wandering alone in the tower. Torin took his hand and pulled him away to go look for a dustpan and broom with him. Sneachta followed; very thankful he didn't have to go alone. The two walked out into the dark hallway. The heavy wooden door creaked as it shut behind them. It reminded Torin of a sinister specter mocking them as they left the safety of Geal's presence. The door became a barrier now that left them out in the coldness of evil and uncertainty. As Torin stood looking up at the door he almost felt as if it were laughing at him.

Slowly Sneachta and Torin walked down the hall looking at doors holding each other's hand tightly. Each door looked as frightening as the one they had just left. Neither wanted to open them to see what was on the other side. Sneachta moved closer to Torins side. He didn't like the feeling in the tower. It was menacing and unwelcoming. As the two walked by a hall table, suddenly a vase fell over and loud screeching ensued. Sneachta tried to scramble up and into Torins coat, but he was far too large by now. The two tumbled to the ground. The screeching continued. Looking up Torin saw a rat scurrying across the tabletop looking for a way down where it could run to safety. 'It's a rat!' Torin exclaimed. Sneachta suddenly reared his head and looked at the frightened creature. He realized they had startled it when they were walking past the table. For an instant Sneachta forgot his fear and instinct took over. In a flash the rat vanished and the screeching stopped. Torin watched as Sneachta quickly gobbled up the rat. When he was done, Sneachta smiled at Torin with a wily grin and merely said, "Comfort food." Torin felt sorry for the rat. It had just been trying to escape. But he also understood that a dragon will eat just about anything that moves. They were not much different from a barn cat when it came to food.

When Torin and Sneachta came to the end of the hall, they saw a small alcove in the wall. Back in the far corner in the shadows was a broom and dustpan. Relieved their hunt was now over, Torin went to grab them.

"What?" Sneachta asked. Torin turned to look at Sneachta.

"What?" Torin asked in return.

"I thought you said something." Sneachta replied. Torin looked blankly at the dragon.

"No, I didn't say anything." Torin said.

Sneachta shrugged. "I guess I was just hearing things. I thought I heard you call my name." Sneachta said.

As Torin went to grab the dustpan and broom once more he felt a slight chilling breeze. Though it was barely audible he thought for a moment he heard faint laughter. But as he turned his head to listen again it was gone.

"This is such a creepy place!" Torin said feeling a little frightened again. Grabbing the broom and dustpan, the two quickly hurried back to Geal.

While Torin and Sneachta had been gone, Geal, Micheál, and Alsandar had gone through the room, examining all the nightmare tapestries. "These are magic tapestries," Geal said, "In each of them are some ones real nightmares."

"So what do we do about it?" Alsandar asked.

"This!" Geal replied, and reaching out with her hand, a white light shot forth, and the tapestry fell into ash.

Alsandar and Micheál looked at the pile of ash on the floor. "Does the nightmare still go on even with the tapestry destroyed?" Alsandar asked.

"No, it's over. Poor thing, whoever the nightmare belongs to," Geal replied.

"So all we gotta do is burn the tapestries, then," Micheál said with a grin, and he went to grab the next tapestry to pull it down.

"Stop! Don't touch it!" Geal cried. Micheál stopped just as he was about to grab the edge of the tapestry. Surprise, he turned to look at Geal and saw her face had turned even paler then it had been before. Micheál didn't think it was even possible.

Looking at Geal and then at his hand he had almost touched the tapestry with, Micheál then nervously tucked his hands in his pockets.

"These are magic tapestries, Micheál. They are alive. Don't touch any of them. They will pull you in forever."

After coming all that way and surviving the impossible, Alsandar felt very unsettled that he had almost lost his brother to a silly folly. Just then Sneachta and Torin came back into the room with the broom and dustpan.

"Now what?" Torin asked as he handed the broom to Geal.

"Don't touch anything, Torin!" Micheál and Alsandar yelled in unison.

Torin and Sneachta both jumped at the sudden yell. "Why?" Torin asked.

"Because Dorcha's black magic is still around, especially in the tapestries. They'll suck you in!" Alsandar answered.

"Does that mean everything!" Torin cried in surprise as he looked at the broom in his hand and threw it to the floor.

Geal chuckled. "Don't worry, I think the broom is safe," she said smiling as she snapped her fingers and the broom flew up into her hand. Geal swept the room with her magic and found all the dark magic things Dorcha had left behind. One by one she turned them and the tapestries to ashes and swept them up herself all the while putting the ashes into a large magic cloth sack. She didn't want to take the chance of any remaining magic harming the brothers or Sneachta. Once the room had been cleaned, Geal went to the next one and would continue to do so until she had cleaned out the tower.

Dorcha had many tapestries. Every room had every inch of wall covered by them. Dorcha had large ones and small ones and even pillow covers, ornate blankets, and furniture shams woven into nightmares. In one room Geal found Dorcha's spinning wheel and loom from which she spun the dark threads and weaved the nightmares. Each and every thing, Geal turned to ash. Geal was becoming tired of them. But it had to be done. As Queen Faerie, only she and other faerie royals had the power to get rid of dark faerie magic. The brothers and Sneachta stood by feeling useless, watching Geal. They wished there was something they could do. But instead they made her tea and snacks and kept her company, talking about each other's lives. Geal learned a great deal about the brothers' family and their parents. She was very impressed with the brothers' mother, Maelíosa. Gifted women such as she were rare. Maelíosa was a healer and possibly a sorceress like her son. Geal was certain Maelíosa was a magical creature herself. Though the work Geal had been doing was wearisome, she was also enjoying the companionship with the brothers. She now understood how Sneachta had grown so attached to them. For the first time, Geal didn't feel so lonely. Her coldness didn't seem to bother them any. No one else stayed in her presence for very long unless they were snow creatures such as her. Geal was going to enjoy having the brothers in her life.

Chapter 15

When Geal had worked her way down to the last floor above the dungeon level, they found a secret library. In the room were also oils and colored powder Dorcha had made into paint. She had been illustrating nightmares and turning them into books as well as weaving them. The shelves were filled with hundreds of books, all filled with nightmares. Some were heinous and horrific, and others were more bland and just plain uncomfortable. Dorcha had been around for hundreds of years and had amassed plenty of nightmares in her time. Other shelves held both ancient and newly written books of magic. On one shelf Alsandar drooled as he saw ancient texts of faerie magic. It was a sorcerer's dream come true. Micheál had already found a book called *The Secrets of the Ancient Ones*, which told the real history of dragons. Curling up in an overstuffed wing chair, Micheál forgot about everyone else in the room. The book held him captivated. Micheál was dumbfounded to learn dragons had been around far longer than anyone else. They had been the original rulers of the earth long before men, faeries, or any creatures came to be. But what delighted Micheál most of all was that the myth of the Valley of the Dragon was true. It had been the breeding grounds of the great dragons long before humans came to be. Far under the layers of time, deep in the earth of the valley, Micheál knew laid the bones of the ancient ones.

By the time Geal had finished the room and all the other rooms on the second to the last floor of the tower, she had grown very tired of the cleaning. She watched the brothers going through the books she had not destroyed. She had finished the cleansing of the level of the tower they were on and decided it was a good time to take a break. She would let the brothers enjoy their newfound knowledge while she rested. All that remained was the dungeon. Geal wasn't too sure what they would find there. She hoped it would not be very dark. Her magic had become drained to the point that all she wanted to do was sleep. Morning would be a good time to start again. It would be the winter solstice, an auspicious day for the final end to centuries of the dark faeries evil.

Alsandar was laughing as he stood at the top of the tower waving his wand through the air. As he did so, sparkles of light shot out at the wand's tip and flew in every direction. As the sparkles went forth, they turned into miniature dragons of every color. Every once in a while, Micheál would grab one from the air and hang on to it. The little dragons then grew rapidly into full-size great dragons. Alsandar watched as Micheál jumped on their backs to fly them around and then land where he would grab another little dragon and repeat the same process over and over. Micheál and Alsandar were thoroughly enjoying themselves. Slowly, Alsandar became aware of a chilly breath on the back of his neck. He dropped his wand to his side and turned around but saw nothing. As he turned back to make more dragons again, he not only felt the cold breath but equally cold hands grab his upper arm. Alsandar looked but again saw nothing. He wasn't afraid since he could see nothing, yet he was very confused as to what it could be. He watched as his sleeves compressed as the invisible hand moved down his arm where it dug deep into his flesh. Alsandar flinched. Startled, he looked around him once more. His arm started to burn where the invisible hand had scratched him. Somewhere deep in his mind Alsandar knew something was wrong. He turned to look at Micheál enjoying himself with the magic dragons, and the scene before him faded to black. He slowly began to realize he had been dreaming. As he rose to consciousness, he found the burning on his arm was still there. Alsandar opened his eyes. He had curled up in front of the fireplace with a book on faerie magic in the library and had fallen asleep. Someone had covered him with a warm blanket. Alsandar sat up and looked down on his arm. His cloak and shirt sleeves were still intact, but his arm still burned. He worried that maybe he had slept to close to the fire, but when he lifted his sleeves to look, he saw three red marks running down his arm. He really had been scratched by something.

Alsandar looked around. The fire had died down low, and the rest of the room was very dark. Micheál was laid out under warm covers on the sofa with a book lying open on his chest. He, too, had fallen asleep reading. Torin was curled up in the big chair next to him peacefully sleeping. He knew Geal and Sneachta had gone up to the top of the tower to sleep where it was cold and comfortable for Geal. But who had scratched him? Everyone was sleeping. Suddenly Alsandar caught a quick movement behind the couch Micheál was sleeping on. As he looked, he thought he saw a shadow figure. The shadow paused to look back at Alsandar and then vanished down through the floor. Alsandar thought he heard the faint sound of a woman laughing. Startled, Alsandar jumped up and ran to where the shadow had vanished. There was nothing there. Alsandar looked around the great room. Nothing else moved. He glanced over at the chamber door, but it was still closed. Nothing had touched it, or Alsandar would have heard it. The door was large and made of heavy wood with a metal latch, braces, and hinges. He would have heard it open if the shadow figure had gone through the door. As Alsandar's arm continued to burn, he became sick to his stomach. Quickly looking around, he found an ornamental pot and threw up in it. His knees then became very weak, and both the pot and Alsandar went crashing to the floor. The crash instantly woke up his brothers who jumped up and looked for the source of the crashing sound. The many past weeks' traveling in the cold wild had taught them to be aware even when they slept.

"There!" shouted Torin as he looked over at the sound of moaning on the floor. There was just enough light to see Alsandar bent over a pot on the floor. Micheál ran over to Alsandar and crouched down beside him.

"Are you okay?" Micheál asked as he lifted his brother's head up. But Alsandar just moaned. "Torin, get the fire going again!" Micheál ordered as he took Alsandar back to lay him down in front of the fireplace. Once the fire was going strong again, the brothers had more light to see Alsandar was feverish and dripping with perspiration. "What happened?" Micheál asked. He was worried that maybe something in the room had gotten to him, something that Geal might have missed. Alsandar moaned again. His head was spinning, and now his stomach burned just like his arm. Alsandar managed to lift his arm and pull up his sleeves.

"Shadow," Alsandar murmured. And then he could say no more. He was feeling so sick and in great pain that he wished for death. He felt certain it would come soon.

Micheál and Torin looked at Alsandar's arm in horror. "What is that?" Torin asked.

"Hurry! Run and get Geal!" Micheál cried. As Torin ran out the door, Micheál grabbed his brother's pack and dug through it. He found his mother's ointment. There was very little of it left. But Micheál scraped out what he could and applied it to Alsandar's arm. The red welts started to fizzle, and bubbly puss came up from the scratches. Micheál wasn't sure what it meant, but he hoped it meant the ointment was dragging out whatever poison had taken Alsandar. As the seconds ticked by while Micheál anxiously waited for Geal, thoughts of his parents went through his head. They had gone so far, went through so much, and were now so close to home again. He hoped it wouldn't all end this way. He hoped for a happy ending after all. As Micheál wiped the beads of sweat from his brother's face Geal had finally come.

Torin had quickly awakened Sneachta and Geal while crying for them to hurry. He had said something had scratched Alsandar. Torin had at least been able to tell her that much as they ran down the tower stairs. The look of terror on Torin's face was enough to tell Geal something was terribly wrong. Since they were in Dorcha's tower, Geal didn't want to waste time questioning Torin. She immediately ran down the stairs. "What happened?" Geal asked as she flew into the room.

"All Alsandar said was 'Shadow,'" Micheál said, and he pointed to Alsandar's arm. Geal lifted his arm and looked at the scratches. As Geal knelt and looked at the festering welts, she understood what had happened.

"It was a shadow creature, a daemon," Geal said.

"A what?" Micheál and Torin shouted together.

"A shadow daemon," Geal replied. "What's this?" Geal asked as she looked closer at Alsandar's arm. There was a green slime dripping with the ooze.

"Oh, that's my mom's ointment," Micheál explained.

"Good work, Micheál! It has bought him some time," Geal said.

"Bought him some time? What do you mean?" Micheál asked worried.

"The shadow daemon has tried to claim his soul. His poison quickly enters the body and turns it dark. But we can stop it. You gave him some extra time, slowed it down some," Geal answered. "Quickly now!" Geal shouted as she rose and started to move all the furniture back. Torin and Micheál jumped up and cleared the floor in haste. Sneachta fluttered above and watched. He was still confused. It had all happened so fast. He had never heard of a shadow daemon before. Sneachta flew toward the fireplace to escape the darkness. He was truly frightened now of all the shadows in the room. "Grab all the candles you can find and light up the room!" Geal commanded. Although Sneachta was very frightened, he helped anyway. He was quicker than the brothers. He could light the candles with his breath as he found them. Geal had drawn a large circle on the floor and placed Alsandar within it. She then threw open a window and with her magic flew in a block of snow. With her magic words she imprinted a sacred blessing on the snow and melted it over Alsandar's body. Alsandar moaned and cried as the blessed water sizzled on his body.

Geal circled around and around the outside of the circle, chanting in her ancient tongue. The brothers and Sneachta watched with rapidly beating hearts, hoping they were in time to save Alsandar. At first nothing seemed to happen, but Geal didn't stop. Around and around she walked, never stopping, always chanting. Finally after what seemed an eternity to the watchers, Alsandar's body started to jerk. Geal's words intensified, and then she stopped. Reaching out with her hand as if she were grabbing something invisible, she closed her fist and threw it toward the fireplace. Suddenly out from Alsandar's body, a dark shadow emerged and went crashing into the flames. The fire roared up and shot out from the fireplace. Everyone quickly ducked down. A strange, bloodcurdling scream came from the flames and died out as the fire died down.

Alsandar lay still while Geal, Sneachta, and Alsandar's brothers looked on. Geal held her hand out to stop Alsandar's brothers from running to his side. "Wait!" Geal exclaimed. Torin anxiously walked around the outside of the circle. Alsandar began to moan a little, and then he turned over on his side. When he opened his eyes, he saw the rest were watching him. Slowly Alsandar sat up.

"What happened?" Alsandar asked.

"Are you okay?" Micheál cried, using all his willpower to keep from running to Alsandar.

"I'm okay, I guess. A bit stiff but okay," Alsandar replied.

"Can you get up and walk?" Geal asked. Alsandar tried but stumbled at first. He tried again and managed to stand on his feet. "Come here, but don't cross out of the circle," Geal commanded. Confused, Alsandar did as she bid. When he stood in front of Geal, she reached out and touched him with her hand. A white light came forth from her fingers, encircling and permeating Alsandar's body. Alsandar smiled.

"That feels good," Alsandar said.

"Let me see your eyes," Geal said. Alsandar looked at her. Then Geal smiled and said, "You're fine. Come out of the circle." Micheál and Torin ran to Alsandar and hugged him. Sneachta squealed with delight and fluttered around them.

"I was so afraid we had lost you, Alsandar," Micheál said.

"I know the feeling," Alsandar chuckled.

Alsandar cringed when Geal explained just how dire his predicament had been. The thought of being trapped in an evil shadow-world sent his mind reeling. He would rather be eaten by a wyvern than suffer in that kind of hell. Geal was still not happy about the situation even though Alsandar was saved. "There remains the matter of the dungeon. If that shadow daemon had come from there, and I think it did since Alsandar said it went through the floor, then we have a particularly nasty clean up job to do yet!" Geal said with disdain. "I will need your help with this one," Geal added. "I will return shortly," Geal said and then turned. She became a cold misty wind and blew out of the window into the dark night. Sneachta closed the window behind her, and the brothers turned to the fireplace to warm up after Geal had left the air chilly behind her. As the brothers sat and stared at the fire wondering what Geal was up to, Torin's stomach gave out a low growl.

When everyone turned to look at him, Torin coyly grinned. "I'm hungry!" he exclaimed.

"I thought it was another shadow daemon," Micheál teased.

"No, just a stomach daemon," Torin quietly replied.

Chapter 16

While the brothers waited for Geal to return, they had a very early breakfast which consisted of a small piece of bread for each. Luckily Torin had kept a chunk of bread in his pocket for a snack. This they divided up equally between them. Their supply food had been left back at the loch when Geal had rescued them from their frozen death. Sneachta had to go scrounging for rats. He didn't mind in the least. The hunt was a fun game for the little dragon. One which he thoroughly enjoyed. The sun was not due to come up for a few more hours, yet the chilling event that happened to Alsandar had them all wide awake and alert. They could not go back to sleep, anyway, with shadow daemons roaming around. The shadows had to be dealt with as soon as possible; there would be no sleeping in the tower until then.

After eating, the brothers roamed through the left-over library. Micheál came upon a very interesting book. It was the book of faerie families. The brothers and Sneachta looked through the names of the different branches of families and were astonished about how far back they went. Toward the end of one particular branch of earth faeries was an insert titled "Wayward Faeries." These were faeries who had crossed the forbidden line and fell in love with humans. In the list, Alsandar recognized a name.

It was his great-grandmother's name. "Micheál, look!" Alsandar cried out.

"What?" Micheál asked.

"It's Nana Brèagha's name!" Alsandar replied.

"Nana?" Micheál replied, deeply surprised.

"Who's Nana Brèagha?" Torin asked.

"She is your great-grandmother, Torin. You never met her. You weren't born yet when she died," Alsandar answered.

"Did you meet her?" Torin asked.

"A few times. But she lived far away and kept to herself mostly. We didn't see her much, but Mom knew her pretty well, I think," Micheál replied.

"Is she a faerie?" Torin asked.

"No, but it says she married one here."

"Wow, I guess that makes us part-faerie!" Alsandar said with a big grin.

"It says here she married a summer earth faerie called Grian Feur," Micheál said.

"Did you ever meet him?" Torin asked.

"No, we never met him, never saw him," Alsandar replied.

Micheál sat back and thought a bit. It explained why his mother was so talented with herbs and plants. She had a gift that went beyond any other healers and herbalists he had ever known of. It explained why his little brother Torin could easily use magic without any training at all. It also crossed Micheál's mind that his brother Alsandar wasn't really a sorcerer after all but more of a magical creature like a faerie instead. He didn't know how the idea would go over with Alsandar since becoming a great sorcerer was all he thought about. Micheál decided to keep his realizations to himself for the time being. He also wondered how much the faerie blood had affected him as well. He had never shown any signs of being magical like his brothers or mother, but he did admit that all his life, he had been drawn to dragons. Perhaps that was his link to his faerie heritage.

"Are our names in there?" Torin asked as he peered over his brother's shoulder to get a closer look.

"No, it seems the faerie line came to an end with Grian Feur. I guess they don't like to list humans mixed in with theirs," Alsandar replied. "I wonder if Grian Feur is still around," Alsandar said.

Suddenly the window whipped open, and a cold mist blew in. Startled, the brothers raised, ready to run, but the mist then quickly transformed into Geal. "I'm back. Here, put these on," Geal said as she whisked around the three, handing them each a necklace with a silver snowflake inscribed with faerie runes. "They're magic talismans. They'll help protect you," Geal explained. The brothers had all but forgotten their new knowledge of their family history with Geal's dramatic entrance. "Well, let's get crackin!" Geal said as she held out her hands, clasped them together, and cracked her knuckles. She was ready to clean house once and for all. She didn't like the daemons. In fact she felt a great amount of pleasure extricating them back to their world. If she had to, she wouldn't mind destroying a few either. Geal sent everyone to get all the candles they could find in the upper rooms where Geal had cleaned and sealed them from anything evil.

Once everyone had returned back to the room, Geal inscribed each and every candle with magic runes of light and protection. The brothers watched with intense awe and interest as each candle Geal inscribed lit up as if made from pure light, and then when she was finished with it, they returned once again to looking like normal candles. When she was satisfied her work was complete, she divided the candles into pouches and handed each a bag of the candles and turned to go out the door. "Follow me, but be very quiet, and stay close!" Geal said as she led them out of the room and down the hall to the dungeon stair well. "Oh, I forgot. If you see anything dark, say these words: 'Beannachd Solas!'" Geal said as they began their descent to the dungeon. "It means Blessed Light." Geal explained.

The closer they came to the bottom of the stairs, the more the air became stale and heavy. They descended without light so their presence would not become known. The darkness below them was oppressive. The ancient stone steps were well worn from centuries of use and slimy from the dripping of water that seeped below ground through the cracks in the dungeon walls. Torin felt himself slipping a few times, so he reached out to grasp the wall to catch his balance. Most places on the wall were slimy, and Torin recoiled at the touch. In some places Torin felt soft moss growing on the wall, which he used to wipe his hands on or grasp when a step was too slippery. He wondered how Dorcha had managed to make her trips down these dark and slimy stairs. Before they descended the last few bottom steps, Geal stopped and held her hand up to stop the others. "Do you feel it?" Geal whispered.

"Feel what?" Micheál asked back as quietly as he could.

"The darkness," Geal answered.

The brothers could feel nothing but the fear and apprehension within their own hearts. Feeling silly he could not feel what Geal felt, Micheál replied, "No, but I can see it." The darkness below them was heavy and oppressive. That he could not mistake. Micheál wondered if that was what Geal actually meant. Geal gave him a funny look.

"Look deep into the darkness below us and reach out with your feelings," Geal whispered. Micheál did as Geal said. As he felt into the darkness, it became something even more. It wasn't just the lack of light he was experiencing but something else in the darkness that made it seem quite dangerous as well as very, very black. It was a presence of some kind, a presence that made him want to turn around and run away.

"There's something really evil down there!" Micheál said.

"Yes," replied Geal smiling, "You're learning. Everyone, do what Micheál has done. You will need this to guide you," Geal whispered a little louder so the rest could hear her. Sneachta tried, and it came very easily to him, but he could also see in the darkness better than the rest.

After being satisfied with testing everyone on their ability to feel in the darkness, Geal took them down the rest of the steps and on to the dungeon floor. Sneachta almost gasped in surprise. It wasn't just a dungeon but a huge cavernous maze of vaulted rooms. The ceiling was high, and he could just make out many other rooms and spaces beyond the one they were in that seemed to go on forever. It was much larger than the outside of the tower might have suggested. "We could get lost down here," Sneachta whispered.

"What do you mean?" Torin asked.

"My eyes are better than yours; I can see how far it goes. It is huge, like a maze!" Sneachta answered.

"How far does it go?" Alsandar asked.

"I don't know, but it goes on and on and on! There are rooms beyond rooms beyond rooms," Sneachta answered. Geal was disappointed. She could also see as Sneachta saw. It would be a bigger job than she first thought. She didn't know how many shadow daemons were down here. She also knew there was something else from the feeling she had, something much more ominous than a shadow daemon.

With the maze of rooms, it seemed to be an overwhelming task. Geal hoped it would not be hard to find them all and there were not too many hiding places in the shadows of the dungeon. She hoped they had enough magic candles to clean out the place.

"So what do we do now?" Micheál asked.

"I'm thinking," Geal answered.

Suddenly from the corner of his eye, Micheál saw a shadow move. He turned to look, and it was gone. "I think I saw one," Micheál whispered.

"Where?" Alsandar asked.

"Over there," replied Micheál pointing to a niche in the wall two feet from where he was standing.

"That is way too close," Alsandar said. The three boys looked at Geal, feeling great anxiety. It was all Torin could do to keep from running back up the stairs. He yearned for the outdoors with its fresh air and sunlight. Sneachta gently took Torin's hand as if he could sense his discomfort. Torin suddenly felt better remembering that Sneachta was there with him as he held his hand.

A dragon is a good thing to have in a dangerous situation, thought Torin. He felt much stronger now.

Geal was certain the shadows knew they were there and that it would not be long before many more came. "Well, they know we are here now, so there's nothing to do about it," Geal said. Taking a candle from her pouch, Geal took one and broke it in half. "Watch me," Geal said. The brothers watched in horror as Geal disappeared into the darkness. Geal had found her way to the center of the room they were in. Taking a half candle, she placed it on the stone floor and lit it. As the flame took hold, she said the words "Beannachd Solas!" Suddenly a circle of glowing light formed on the stone below the candle, and the room lit up as if the sun were shining up from the floor. The room was no longer dark but full of light as bright as a sunny day. Moans and screeching could be heard as the shadows receded from the room. Geal walked back to the brothers and Sneachta. "We'll have to split up and do each room as we go. We'll drive them back to the last room," Geal explained.

Torin grew frightened at the thought of leaving the comfort and security of the group. He didn't want to leave his brothers. Micheál and Alsandar also felt panicked at the thought of going through the dark rooms without the rest of the group. They didn't want what happened to Alsandar to happen to any others as well.

"What happens if they get to us before we reach the center of a room?" Micheál asked in a terrified voice.

"Just keep the magic talismans I gave you tucked down in your shirts and remember the words I told you. If you do as I say, you'll be fine," Geal replied.

Micheál hoped she was right.

"Why keep them in our shirts?" Alsandar asked.

"So the shadows can't rip them off you." Geal answered. "They'll try anything to stop you."

The group split up. Geal went off on her own while Torin went with Sneachta because of his good eyes, and Micheál went with Alsandar who had magic for his defense. Frightened to begin with, Torin felt the magic talismans under his shirt and quietly repeated the words Geal had taught them over and over as he walked along. The charm glowed warm and bright under his shirt. Torin felt relief, renewed strength, and courage when he looked down and saw the light of his talisman coming through the fabric of his shirt. The next few rooms went quite easily. Each group could see the next room lit up and glowing. It gave the brothers and Sneachta a deep sense of relief to be in a place of light. The lit rooms threw light into the next—enough for them to see farther in the dark rooms they entered. As they cleared each of the vaulted rooms, their courage grew.

All along the way, the screams and moans of the shadow creatures could be heard as they fled the light. "This is easier than I thought it would be," Alsandar commented.

"Yeah!" Micheál said as he fearlessly strode into the next room and walked toward the center stone in the floor. Micheál reached his destination when he suddenly felt his legs get kicked out from under him. He hit the stone floor with a loud thump. As he looked up all he could see were shadow-like creatures with red glowing eyes and black shiny teeth snarling at him. From out of the darkness Micheál and Alsandar heard a woman laughing. Micheál felt a cold chilly breeze brush up against the side of his face as if it were kissing his cheek. "Micheál." the voice whispered, "I am coming for you." The laughing started up again and then died off as Micheál felt claws tearing at his clothes. "Alsandar!" Micheál screamed, feeling terror and panic freeze him helplessly where he lay.

"Beannachd Solas!" Alsandar yelled as he quickly lit a candle and placed it on the floor next to Micheál. The dark shadows screamed in pain as the light shot forth around them. The brothers watched in shock as the shadows disintegrated before their eyes and their screams faded into nothingness. "You okay?" Alsandar asked as he bent down to help his brother stand up. Micheál stood and examined his body. He didn't feel any burning or scratches, but his clothes were ripped to shreds. His magic talisman glowed brightly under the tears of his clothing. Micheál sighed in relief. It had indeed protected him.

"Yes, I think I'm okay," Micheál replied.

"You have to be more careful, Micheál. We can't just go charging into the darkness like that," Alsandar scolded. Micheál felt ashamed of himself. It had all been going so easy. He realized he had fallen into a false sense of security.

"Did you hear that voice?" Micheál asked.

"Yes." Alsandar replied.

"I wonder what it was." Micheál said. Alsandar shrugged.

"I don't know Micheál, probably one of the shadow daemons." Alsandar answered.

"I didn't know they talked." Micheál said. "You ready for the next one?" Alsandar asked.

"Just give me a minute," Micheál replied as he crouched down to relieve his weak shaky legs and rested his head against his clasped hands. He closed his eyes and felt himself still trembling. It had been a close call. He needed to regain his wit.

Sneachta looked beyond the lighted room into the next and scrutinized the darkness for any movement. He could see none. But Sneachta knew the shadows were there. He had no doubt they were waiting for their chance to attack them. Scanning the room again, he could see the center of the room from where he stood. "Okay, I don't see anything moving," Sneachta said.

Torin then took Sneachta's clawed fingers in his hands and crept toward the center of the room. With his other hand, he grasped the talisman through his shirt and quietly repeated, "Beannachd Solas!" over and over again. Sneachta then caught with his eyes the shadows close by move away. Sneachta could feel Torin shaking as he held his hand.

Clasping Torin's hand tighter Sneachta whispered, "I'm here, Torin. I won't let them get you." Torin and Sneachta reached the center of the room and placed a candle on the floor. Sneachta quickly lit it with his fiery breath while Torin chanted the magic words. The room immediately filled with light. With the lighting of each candle, they could hear the shrieks of the shadows as they disbursed back into the darkness of the next room ahead.

"I hope we're getting close to the end," Torin said as he looked beyond to his next assignment.

"Me too," Sneachta said.

"We are running out of candles," Torin said as he looked through his bag of candles. He only had one and a half candles left. He had been breaking them in half as Geal had ordered. Torin worried that there would not be enough to finish the job. Then an awful idea struck his mind. "Sneachta, what happens when the candles burn down?" Torin asked.

"I don't know," Sneachta answered. He thought of being stuck in the darkness again when all the candles had burned. "When we get down to the last one, let's find Geal," Sneachta said.

"Okay, we have two more rooms then. We'll save the last for when we find Geal. She'll know what to do," Torin said.

Chapter 17

Geal was running short of candles as well. She knew the others would be also. If they didn't have enough they would have to wait to finish the job until they could get more candles. Geal didn't like that. She knew the shadows would be planning a better line of defense while they were gone. Though she knew she could defeat them, she didn't relish the notion of having to fight against them further. She wanted to get the job done and take the brothers back home to see their parents before they settled into the tower. Geal had missed Sneachta and worried about him endlessly. She knew Torin's parents would be going through the same agony, the agony of worrying and not knowing. Geal didn't like that. She didn't like it when she went through it, and she didn't want others to suffer the same awful things she did. Geal hoped they were coming close to the end of the vaults as she glanced into the darkness of the next one. Beyond that she saw a light come on in the fault next to it. The candle lighters were getting closer together now. Sighing in relief, Geal knew they were indeed coming to the end of the vaults.

Torin had just lit the second to the last of his candles when he heard footsteps behind him. He didn't know shadows made noises when they walked. Up until now they had been very quiet. Startled, Torin jumped up and turned around, grasping his talisman tightly in his fingers shouting over and over, "Beannachd Solas!" Torin lit up like a large candle.

"It's just Alsandar and Micheál," Sneachta said, relieved it wasn't a shadow creature.

"You're a bit jumpy!" Alsandar said as he smiled down at Torin who was slowly losing his glow now.

"You scared me!" Torin exclaimed.

"We were just in the next room. We saw your light go on," Alsandar said.

"We're out of candles. Well, except one," Micheál said.

"Me too," Torin replied.

"So we're going to find Geal and see what she wants us to do," Alsandar said.

"We were going to do the same thing," Sneachta replied.

Suddenly Torin noticed Micheál's ripped clothing. "What happened to you?" Torin asked.

"Oh, I ran into a few bad ones. But I'm fine," Micheál replied.

"Yeah! You should have seen it! All teeth and red glowing eyes. They chewed him up!" Alsandar said. Torin and Sneachta recoiled in fear. They could now see looking at Micheál how bad the shadows could be. Alsandar chuckled as he watched Torin and Sneachta looking at Micheál's tattered clothes. Micheál glared at Alsandar. He didn't think it was funny.

"Okay, so I was stupid, and that is how they got me. But we kicked their butts!" Micheál exclaimed with a wily grin.

"They just up and disintegrated when the light hit them. It kills them!" Alsandar said. "Wanna see?" Alsandar asked.

"What?" Torin cried, terrified. "No I don't!" Torin hated it when his brothers teased him. He hoped Alsandar was doing just that, teasing him. After the sight of Micheál, Torin didn't think it was worth taking a chance to do it again.

"I don't, either, Alsandar! Once is enough!" Micheál scolded with anger in his eyes as he looked at Alsandar.

"I was just teasing!" Alsandar recoiled.

The brothers and Sneachta made their way through the lighted rooms. As they glanced around them, they noticed the lighted rooms went in a circle. The vaulted dungeon was round. When they came to the last room lit, they found Geal. She too had only one candle left. "So what do we do now?" Micheál asked as Geal looked at her last half of candle she held in her hand. Geal raised an eyebrow as she looked up and saw Micheál's tattered clothing.

Micheál shyly backed away behind his brother Alsandar who grinned at Geal waiting for her to ask what had happened, but Geal just looked away and said, "I'm not sure just yet." Geal looked around the vaulted rooms that stretched one beyond the other. "It seems this place is a giant circle. We have been herding the shadows into the center of the dungeon," Geal said. "I think we may be close to the last ones, though, judging from the lighted rooms we have so far." The brothers looked around at all the lighted rooms. They had to be getting close, just as Geal said. From what they could see, there would not be space enough in the dungeon for many more rooms in the circle.

Geal walked through the lighted rooms next to the center dark ones. "I count three that have no light, and the next after must be the center room," Geal said.

"It is strange how dark they can be with so much light coming from the other rooms. I mean, the entrances are wide open and really don't have a door, so wouldn't the light from one brighten the next somehow?" Alsandar asked.

"Normally I would think so," Geal said, "but the darkness in them isn't a normal darkness. It is *the* darkness you see."

"No, I can't. It's too dark." Alsandar giggled.

Geal smiled and gently popped him on the nose. "Such a silly boy," Geal replied. "Well, we have three rooms and three candles left. Let's light them up," Geal said.

"Geal, what happens when the candles burn out?" Torin asked feeling worried as Geal started off to the next dark room.

Geal turned and smiled at him. "Don't worry, Torin, they stay lit. They have magic runes on them. As the candle melts, the runes melt into the floor and become a part of them sealing out any evil forever. And as it is day outside, so it is in here, and when the moon shines, so it does in here," Geal explained.

"Wow!" Torin exclaimed, "You could grow things in here, couldn't you, just like outside?" Micheál stopped walking and turned around while looking at all the lighted rooms. It did look like day light down under the ground in the dungeon.

"You know, Mom would love this! She could grow all her herbs down here all year long," Micheál said.

With three candles left, Geal instructed the brothers and Sneachta to light the last three rooms. The shadows growled fiercely and reached out to rip at the brothers in one last attempt to hold their ground. But each brother recited the magic words as they clutched their talismans, forcing the shadows to flee to the center room of darkness. One by one, the rooms lit up bright as day. As the group tried to peer across the center room to try to see the light across from them, they were met with darkness. When they came together once again, no one said a word. They looked into the darkness in front of them and wondered what would meet them there. "Now what?" Micheál asked.

"I don't know for sure yet. Let me think," Geal replied. Torin and Sneachta settled down on the floor and looked around them. Torin thought of his mother and how much she really would love to live in a place like this. She could have her garden back all year round. But then he knew if she were there, he would be the one to help haul down all the dirt she would need for her plants. Then, after a second thought, Torin didn't mind. He would do anything right now to be back with his mother again and to see her smile at him.

While Torin daydreamed about his mother smiling down on him for hauling in all her dirt, the five heard a rattling sound. It was weak at first but then became stronger. It was the sound of chains. Whatever it was, it was either bound by chains or had chains to fight back with. As Torin and Sneachta cautiously stood ready to run if they had to, they heard a growl that became a loud soul-piercing howl. "Who's there?" Geal demanded. All that answered was another howl and then a groan which turned into a whimpering mournful cry. Then after a moment of silence malevolent laughter came from the darkness. It started out low then became loud and deafening and silent again. As they listened further whispering could be heard just beyond the darkness. Then a woman's voice called out, "Micheál! Micheál."

"I've heard that voice before." Geal said.

"Me too." Sneachta said.

"Me three, just a little while ago actually." Micheál added. Micheál stood closer to the darkness to hear better. Geal was paused as well trying to remember where she had heard the voice before. As it suddenly came to her several shadow daemons reached out and dragged Micheál into the darkness.

"It's Dorcha!" Geal cried out.

"What!" Alsandar cried out surprised as he watched his brother vanish into the darkness.

"How can that be? I saw Micheál cut her head off and kill her! We saw her rotting body!" Alsandar exclaimed in a state of panic. Grabbing his talisman in his hand he shouted "Beannachd Solas!" and ran into the darkness.

"Alsandar wait!" Geal shouted after him but he was gone before she could finish her words. Turning to Torin and Sneachta Geal ordered them to fall back and stay put. "We don't need you two in there as well!" Geal scolded as she ran into the darkness also.

Micheál felt his body held tightly in the grasp of many hands. The claws pressed deeply into his flesh. He could not grab a candle let alone even light one. His heart beat rapidly as he realized he had made another stupid mistake. A cold breeze once again brushed up against his face. "Hello Micheál." said a woman's voice. Micheál could see nothing but the darkness. The voice seemed to float all around him. "Who are you?" Micheál demanded.

"Why you know me Micheál. You took my head off." replied the voice. Micheál thought for a moment. *It couldn't be!* He saw Dorcha die, by his own sword. He saw her half-eaten body and the black brambles growing through her bones. "What do you want" Micheál asked.

"Well, what do you think I want? I mean really Micheál!" Dorcha scolded back. Dorcha laughed again as if she were half crazy. Micheál felt icy cold hands grab his jaws and turn his face towards something invisible. "I want...revenge!" Dorcha shouted. Micheál felt a blast of cold air in his face. "You took everything from me Micheál!" Dorcha said.

"You took everything from us first!" Micheál yelled back, "You torched our homes, killed our people, and destroyed the Valley we lived in!"

"Dorcha!" Geal called out as she suddenly came into the darkness. Micheál looked towards her voice and could barely make Geal out in the darkness. Her sparkly winter faerie apparel and crown gave off just a bit of light in the darkness.

"Oh! Hello Geal." Dorcha snidely remarked. "If you've come to destroy me, it's a little too late. Your boy here has already done that." Dorcha said jabbing Micheál into his gut with her claw. Micheál almost fell over from the pain, but the shadow daemons held him firm.

"And yet here you are Dorcha, just a shadow of your former self." Geal said.

Dorcha growled at Geal's insult. "Yes, a shadow now, But I still have power." Dorcha replied with an evil sneer.

"As do I Dorcha." Geal warned. Dorcha laughed again. Geal tried to think of a way to throw Dorcha off guard long enough to get Micheál free of the daemons. Even though Dorcha was but a shadow now, she was still an evil faerie shadow with powers, powers that went beyond the living. Then without warning

Dorcha reached out and grabbed Micheál in the stomach. He yelled out in agony as he felt his life source being ripped from the center of his being.

"NO!" Geal shouted.

Dorcha laughed on. She would rip out his soul and take it with her to the underworld of the shadows. Suddenly there was a flash of light, and for just a few seconds, Dorcha's form could be seen. As she turned to look at the source of light, a shocked look spread across her face. Alsandar stood directly behind her with his talisman shoved firmly through her ghostly body within the center of her being. A warm golden light permeated the three. Alsandar cried out his brother's name and shouted, "I love you Micheál!" Dorcha's head fell back as sheer agony spread across her face. Tiny shafts of white light began appearing all through her form vanquishing her bit by bit till none remained. Her painful cries echoed throughout the darkness and then fell silent. Micheál fell as the daemons around him were also destroyed by Alsandar's light of love. Alsandar grabbed him up right before he hit the floor and quickly dragged him out of the darkness.

Micheál and Alsandar sat on the floor looking back into the darkness. Micheál wondered if what he had just been through had been real. He felt perfectly fine now that it was all over. But what he had felt when Dorcha had a hold of something that went deep inside him was entirely something else. He literally felt his life ripping away in Dorcha's hands.

"Are you ok Micheál?" Alsandar asked on the verge of tears. The whole experience had horrified him. When he ran into the darkness he could see nothing. Then he heard the voices and used them as a guide. He was so relieved to hear Geal had found Micheál as well. He waited for a chance to get Micheál free. Geal's conversation had kept Dorcha occupied as he snuck up behind her. He was sure it would cost him his life but at the moment rescuing his brother was all he could think of. He took a chance that he could stop Dorcha long enough for Micheál to escape.

What happened afterwards was entirely unexpected. Alsandar had no idea his talisman would have the power to destroy Dorcha's shadow spirit. But then as he felt his love for his brother burst forth inside him he felt an immense power of love amplifying the light of the talisman that seemed to melt away all the evil around them. Soon it was all over and they were all free to flee the darkness.

Geal kneeled down beside Micheál and looked him over to make sure he was alright. There were no marks or scars where he had been handled and poked. Micheál seemed to be physically fine. "So, just how exactly did you kill Dorcha Micheál?" Geal asked. Micheál looked up at Geal a little confused. "What do you mean? I simply cut off her head." Micheál replied.

"And did you leave the head with the body?" Geal asked.

Micheál shook his head., "No, I threw it as far as I could. I was very angry."!

"So the head wasn't with the body when the brambles grew?" Geal asked.

"No." Micheál replied.

"Well, then that explains it." Geal said as she too sat back on the floor next to Alsandar and Micheál. Geal went on to explain that when a Fearie was destroyed it was the growth of their element be it plant or mineral that entombed the soul of the faerie. It was returned to it primal natural state of being. In Dorcha's case, her head had escaped. It was the source of her intelligence. Only part of her soul had been entombed.

"Well, is she dead now?" Torin asked.

"Oh yes, she is dead now." Geal replied.

The five sat down together looking into the darkness. All were relieved the ordeal was over. Then a moaning and the rattle of chains could be heard once more in the darkness.

"Hey! I thought you said Dorcha was dead again!" Torin said as he and his brothers quickly scrambled from the edge of darkness into the adjacent lighted room. Geal stood up but did not run. She instead listened to the sounds coming from within the darkness.

Geal paced back and forth a little as she thought. Whatever was in the center darkness didn't sound like it was malevolent; it sounded more tortured and sad to her. But then that would be just what was needed to draw in the shadow creatures.

"There is something else in there, and I don't think it is evil," Geal said.

"What is it?" Alsandar asked.

"I think it is a catalyst," Geal answered.

"What's a catalyst?" Sneachta asked.

"It is things that cause an event, an action, or in this case something that draws in the shadow creatures," Geal replied.

"Why would Dorcha have a catalyst anyway?" Micheál asked.

"Because she is a dark faerie. She deals with nightmares and negative things. A catalyst such as this draws in the negative powers, in this case, the shadow creatures. She needs them to weave her dark magic and mental anguish into her nightmares," Geal answered. "Micheál, Alsandar, go find a couple of buckets and fill them with snow. And hurry," Geal said.

Torin was stunned. "You mean all those tapestries were made from shadow creatures?" Torin asked.

"Yes," Geal answered.

Whoever or whatever was in the center room was a victim of Dorcha. She had put it through immense torture and heartbreak in order to drive it into such a state of agony that the suffering brought what she needed to her. Dorcha was very evil indeed. Geal knew such negative emotions attracted negative energies. She felt very sad for Dorcha's victim. Emotions such as constant sadness, hate, and anger only brought evil into one's life. As it consumed the thoughts and worked its way into the soul, all light was eventually lost and only the darkness remained. Geal hoped whatever dwelled beyond was not above hope. Otherwise, she would have to destroy it as well. This grieved Geal greatly. It would not be fair to Dorcha's victim. To have unjustly suffered through such torment only to be destroyed. Geal doubted that the catalyst even deserved such a punishment to begin with. Geal thought it would be just like Dorcha to take an innocent. Evil didn't care for the goodness as those in the light did. It would not mean much to the dark ones to be tormented; after all, they were dark to begin with. They would not feel the pain of losing the joy of light.

While Micheál and Alsandar were gone on Geal's errand, Sneachta, Torin, and Geal sat on the floor, staring into the darkness. She put her arms around the two and listened to the tortured moaning coming from the darkness before them. Both Sneachta and Torin felt comfort and warmth safe with in Geal's protective arms even though they were held within her icy embrace. "I wonder who it is Dorcha has bound in there," Geal said. Sneachta and Torin wondered too. After a few more minutes of watching the darkness and listening to the tormented cries within it, Geal started to sing. She started out softly then grew louder. Geal had a beautiful voice. Torin was surprised; he didn't know she could sing. Geal sang in an ancient language neither Sneachta nor Torin understood. Geal's voice spread throughout the entire dungeon, echoing off the walls. The sound was very pleasing to Sneachta and Torin. Her song was mournful yet calming at the same time. It reached into Torin's heart where he felt it rolling through his emotions. He felt himself held captivated by her song even if he could not understand its words. Torin finally realized it was a magic song, a song of the faeries. The chains and mournful sounds coming from the darkness ceased. Geal felt the presence within the last chamber listening to her voice. Torin had forgotten about time and could only think of the moment he was now in. For Torin, Geal's song seemed to last forever. She sang until the return of Micheál and Alsandar.

When Micheál and Alsandar had reached the dungeon floor again, they stopped in amazement. The sound of Geal's voice clung to their hearts and pulled them in toward her as it echoed throughout the dungeon. The lighted chambers took on a different light; it was a light that had a glow of its own. The ambiance of the chambers became pure, magical, and sacred. It was as if they had walked into a holy place. The brothers knew they had to hurry, but the song bade them to listen and enjoy instead. The brothers wanted to sit and listen to the song as it filled their hearts with great hope and promise of greater things to come. They felt all the bad things they had been through fall behind into a far and distant past. It was something they had never experienced before. They felt a sort of cleansing of their souls as the song went through their minds. As much as they wanted to sit and let the song run through them, they persevered and made their way back to Geal, entranced by the song. When Geal heard the sound of their footsteps come up from behind her, she stopped singing. "That was beautiful!" Alsandar exclaimed as he sat his bucket down before Geal.

"Shhh, listen," Geal whispered putting a finger to her lips to indicate silence. Micheál and Alsandar listened as Geal commanded. The sound within the darkness was silent. Micheál put his bucket down, and Geal stood up.

The brothers and Sneachta watched as Geal sang another song over the snow. The snow in the buckets started to glow and sparkle as if the sun was shining down upon it. Facing the brothers and Sneachta, Geal indicated complete silence by brushing her index finger across her lips once again. The four stood and watched silently as Geal took the buckets and walked toward the darkness of the center chamber. As Geal stepped into the chamber, she vanished. No one could see her anymore. "Who goes there?" moaned the tortured voice. "Is that you, Dorcha?" the voice asked anxiously.

"No," Geal answered. Suddenly a great many growls and howls erupted in the darkness. The brothers stood back, fearful of the commotion and worried about Geal. Torin and Sneachta clung to each other watching the darkness and hoping Geal would walk out of it soon. Geal had stirred the retreating shadow creatures into action. They came at her in one last attempt to rip her to shreds. But in a flash, Geal tossed the snow from the buckets, and it began to fall all around the chamber of darkness. The snowflakes sparkled as if they were made of pure light. All around, the darkness disappeared, and the shadow creatures screamed in agony. The shadows began to disintegrate as the snowflakes of light hit their shadowy bodies.

The snow within the chamber kept falling until it was dark no more. Geal gasped as she saw the creature before her. It was a faerie that was bound to a silver post with magical runes carved into it. He was aged and diseased. His face was sunken and hallowed while his clothes were nothing but shreds of what use to be complete clothing that hung ragged over his yellowed skin. The bound faerie was hardly a man anymore but a skin-covered skeleton instead that seemed to barely cling to life. He was a pitiful sight. "Oh, you poor thing!" Geal whispered as she approached the faerie. Reaching out, she brushed her hand lovingly against his cheek. The bound faerie began to sob heavily. Geal held the faerie in her icy arms, and the silver post suddenly turned to dust, releasing the faerie who immediately fell. Geal quickly held him up and then gently laid him down on to the floor. Geal then tore off the chains that were wrapped around him. The brothers and Sneachta ran into the chamber when they saw the darkness was gone and Geal leaning over a strange creature that lied on the floor.

"What is that?" Torin asked.

Geal turned to him with a disgruntled expression. "You mean, who is that!" she scolded. Torin felt ashamed. The creature on the floor didn't look like anything he had ever seen before. It didn't look human or even faerie to him. It looked like a shriveled up wrinkled skin covered skeleton to Torin. He didn't think to stop and think. It was a shocking sight.

"I'm sorry," Torin said. "Who is that?" he added softly trying to correct himself.

Geal lifted the weak head of the faerie on the floor to rest in her lap. "Please, sir, what is your name?" Geal softly asked. The faerie turned and look up at her with his large, sorrow-filled eyes.

"I am Grian, or so I am told. Dorcha has screamed that name at me for an eternity. I don't remember anymore if that is true or not. I'm sorry that is all I remember. I have been bound up in here for so long I don't know anything else."

Alsandar gasped. The faerie family history came rushing back into his mind. "Grian? Grian Feur?" Alsandar asked in a loud surprised voice.

"Alsandar, that's our great-grandfather!" Micheál shouted excitedly.

Geal was still looking down on the faerie feeling immense sorrow for what had happened to him. As she heard the name complete, her eyes grew wide in surprise. "Grian, Grian Feur?" Geal asked. "Oh my goodness! We wondered what had happened to you. One day you were here, and the next you had vanished, never to be seen again," Geal said. She had been too surprised by the name herself to really listen to the rest of what Micheál had said. Then suddenly their words hit her like a ton of stone. "Great grandfather? What do you mean great grandfather?" Geal exclaimed, feeling shocked. Micheál and Alsandar explained about the book they had found in Dorcha's library. The two rambled on so quickly and excitedly Geal could hardly make out what they were saying. But as she listened, she put it all together in her mind. She understood. In a state of shock, Geal carefully put Grian's head back down on the floor and slowly stood. Turning, she faced the brothers. "You are of faerie blood?" Geal asked, suddenly looking saddened.

"I guess so," Alsandar replied.

"Then I cannot claim you as mine!"

Chapter 18

It had been an eventful month for Geal. Suddenly she felt weak and tired. She had lost Sneachta, and then he was returned again, Dorcha had been destroyed, and Geal had found a new family in which she had hoped her loneliness was gone forever, and she had also found the long missing faerie only to find out in the end she would lose her newfound family. On top of all that, she felt very drained from all the magic power she had been using for the past two days. It was all too much for Geal to take in all of a sudden.

Grian Feur had lain silently watching the five talk around him. "Please, do you know me?" Grian asked in a weak voice trying to reach out to Micheál with his bony hand. "Tell me if you know who I am."

Alsandar and Micheál bent down next to Grian. Alsandar took Grian's bony hand and gently told him who he was. "Yes, you're our great-grandfather, Grian Feur. You married our great-grandmother Nana Brèagha." Alsandar felt tears well up in his eyes as his heart broke for the man before him on the cold stony floor. Here before him lay a once healthy faerie, his own great-grandfather. He was in such a frightful state, and even though he knew the faerie was kin, the creature didn't seem as if it could be. What evil could have done this? It seemed Dorcha had a long history of destroying his family. Why did Dorcha do this, and how could anyone do anything so terrible to begin with to another living thing?

Grian looked up at Alsandar and saw the compassion in his eyes. Could this young man truly be his great-grandson? Grian thought of the name of the woman he had been given for a moment, but it didn't sound familiar to him. "I'm sorry, I don't remember a Nana," Grian said finding it hard to speak yet in his weakened state.

"Well, actually, we call her Nana because she was our grandmother, but her real name is Aiofa Brèagha," Micheál explained.

Grian rolled his head back to look at the ceiling. His eyes stared blankly as his mind searched and searched for the name in his past. Suddenly a picture of a green and bountiful glen appeared in his mind. He heard the laughter of a young woman. As he turned, he saw her. There before him was a beautiful young woman running and laughing in circles around him as she threw petals of wild flowers at him, and then suddenly it all came crashing back into his memory. Tears once again rolled down from his eyes. "Oh, Aiofa, my darling, beautiful Aiofa," Grain moaned.

Geal had finally composed herself and turned to the brothers. "Let's get him up into the tower and put him into bed. He needs to heal and regain himself now," Geal said.

Grain had been tucked safely into bed and was sleeping peacefully. Geal, Sneachta, and the brothers were in the library looking through the book of faerie families. Geal had wondered what had happened to Grian Feur. He just vanished one summer day, and no one ever heard from him again. But now as she read his name in the book, she wondered if Dorcha had imprisoned him because he had crossed the line and married a human. It would be just like Dorcha to punish someone for such a thing. No one knew Grian had crossed the line. Grian had kept it secret. Maybe Dorcha had found out somehow and took it upon herself to deal out the judgment. It was rare for faeries to do such things but not unheard of. Every once in a while, a faerie was tempted by an unusual human, one who was exceptionally beautiful or talented or, more often, both. But what Dorcha did was uncalled for. Faeries usually understood the power of love, and there wasn't any real punishment for such an act. If such a deed were ever found out, the human was usually taken into the faerie world, and that was the end of it. On rare occasions the human chose to live in both worlds. Rules were different when it came to marriage of human and faerie. The human became part of the faerie family and thus abided by the laws. They were allowed to travel back and forth between worlds just as their spouse did. No one minded though. True love was greatly respected and admired in the faerie world. Geal wondered if there had been something more to why Dorcha had done such a horrible thing to Grian.

Geal walked over to the window and looked at the snow-covered ground outside. The tower had been cleansed of the darkness, and Geal thought of what to do next. Since the brothers had faerie blood in their linage, she could not claim them. She had claimed Dorcha's tower but could not stay there even if she wanted to. In time, spring would come, and she would have to return to her own domain. Both she and Sneachta would have to return home soon, anyway, or her own home would melt in the spring. Perhaps when Grian became strong enough, he might keep the tower for her. But then after all the years of being imprisoned there, he might not want to stay. At least if he did stay with the tower, he would be close to Aiofa's family. Geal turned back and watched the brothers and Sneachta laughing and talking as they looked through the names in the book of faerie families. Geal felt a great sadness within. She would have to return the brothers home, and she would lose her new family. As Geal watched them, she felt an icy teardrop run down her cheek.

Torin looked up to see what Geal was doing and saw the sadness in her face. "What's wrong, Geal? You look so sad," Torin said.

"I am just thinking that when I return you home, I will miss you very much," Geal replied.

"I thought we were going to stay in the tower," Alsandar said feeling very disappointed. He had been looking forward to exploring all the magic books Geal had left in the library.

"I cannot claim you—you have faerie blood. I must return you home," Geal answered sadly. Micheál stood up from his seat on an overstuffed settee he had been sharing with Torin as they looked through the book and walked over to Geal.

"We do want to go home, Geal, but we don't want to leave the tower, either. And we don't want to leave you. If it is all right, can we claim you? Can we stay? Can we be like part of your family as well?" Micheál asked. Geal became overwhelmed with emotion. She covered her mouth with her hand, trying to stifle a cry. More tears fell from her eyes, but they were tears of joy.

"Yes! Yes you can stay, and I don't want to leave you, either," Geal exclaimed.

"But what about Mom and Dad?" Torin asked.

"Well, they can come here with us. Mom will love it!" Alsandar exclaimed, thinking about the dungeon that now shined with both the sun during daylight and the moon light at night.

"I think we should bring Mom here anyway. Grain Feur needs her medicine I think," Torin added. His brothers agreed.

"I think your mother would be happy to finally meet her grandfather," Geal said, glowing with happiness once again.

The tower was a happy place now, and the brothers, Sneachta, and Geal were chatting happily about their plans for the future. Geal was excited she would be able to see the brothers any time she liked. Suddenly Geal thought of something. "It is the winter solstice today! We must get you back to your parents before the sun sets." She felt excitement grow within as she thought of reuniting the sons with their parents. Geal looked out the window. It would not be long from where the sun now hung lower in the sky before the sun set. Cleaning the dungeon had taken most the night and over half the day. It was the winter solstice, and Geal could not think of a better time to return what was lost to the brothers' parents. It would be a wonderful solstice gift. The brother's laughed, danced, and hugged each other joyfully at the realization they were finally going to see their parents once again. So much had happened to them, and they had been gone so long. At times it felt like they would never see their parents again. Torin began to sob heavily as he thought of his mother's arms holding him once more. Micheál took Torin in his arms and rocked him gently as he tried to sooth his tears. "I know, Torin, I know," Micheál said as he stroked Torin's hair and held him tighter.

Geal watched the two for a moment. "Well, what are we waiting for? Let's get you home!" Geal exclaimed with a rather large smile on her face.

After checking on Grian Feur to make sure he was all right, the brothers, Sneachta, and Geal went up to the tower balcony where they had first landed. Calling the wind to her again, Geal protected the brothers from its icy chill and took them all down to the valley below. The wind took them rushing at breathtaking speed over the land below them. The brothers watched in amazement as they rapidly approached the farm the brothers had known as home all their lives. The wind whipped up the snow from the ground below, and the brothers saw a few rooftop shingles fly off as they ascended to the ground. Once they safely landed on the ground, Torin ran toward the front door, calling for his mother and father. The front door swung open, and Maelíosa and Ernst came running out. Maelíosa grabbed up her son in her arms and cried. She swung her son around and around, laughing until Torin's weight threw Maelíosa off balance, sending them rolling in the snow. But they didn't care. Geal watched the happy reunion between the parents and their children. Maelíosa and Torin rose from the wet, snowy tumble. Torin ran to his father while Maelíosa went to her two oldest boys. "I knew you would bring him home," Maelíosa said as she hugged her two older sons.

Micheál and Alsandar grinned, feeling very proud of themselves for keeping their promise to their mother.

Maelíosa and Ernst finally noticed the strange and beautiful woman with a small white dragon next to her standing by quietly watching them. "This is Geal Geamhradh, the winter queen," Micheál said.

"I know," his father replied, awestruck. Maelíosa and Ernst bowed down in the snow in front of Geal.

"Thank you for returning our sons home," Maelíosa said.

The winter queen frowned and replied, "Well…about that." Geal wasn't sure how they would take the news of the tower as she looked around at the carefully tended farm. Geal knew it had taken a lot of work and that Maelíosa and Ernst might not want to leave it.

Before Geal could explain her words, Maelíosa's great joy suddenly turned to a horrible cold fear that went rushing through her body. She knew full well that once a human found the realms of the faeries, they could never come back again. Standing up in disbelief and shock, she cried out, "No!" and ran toward the winter queen to beg her to let her keep her sons. Ernst ran for his wife and caught her in his arms before she could touch the robes of the winter queen. No human had ever touched the winter queen before, and he didn't know what would happen.

Being unable to beg, Maelíosa turned to Ernst and began sobbing in her husband's arms. He held her tightly and cried with her. He could not bear the thought of never seeing his sons again. A great sadness took over the joyful homecoming. As Maelíosa and Ernst cried in each other's arms, Sneachta crept up and tugged on Maelíosa's tunic. "It's okay, Mom. Why are you crying? They are home."

Maelíosa looked down at Sneachta. "Mom?" she asked rather coarsely through her tears as she thought of how her sons now belonged to the winter queen and were no longer hers.

Embarrassed, Sneachta stepped back and explained, "I do not know your name. My friends only call you Mom. So I call you Mom because that is the only name I know for you." Sneachta had completely misunderstood Maelíosa's response. Geal Geamhradh wanted to hold Maelíosa and comfort her, but she knew it would only chill her instead. In haste to ease the grief before her eyes, Geal Geamhradh stepped forward and quickly explained she would not claim Maelíosa's sons.

Geal felt her own tears falling to the ground as tiny droplets of ice. She understood the pain Maelíosa felt. She had been through the same thing with Sneachta missing. "I grieve with you. My heart broke for you, but now all is well," Geal said with a tearful smile. "I'm sorry I wasn't clear to begin with. I should have spoken differently."

Maelíosa looked back into the face of Geal and saw her sincerity. "Will you come in for some tea?" Maelíosa asked, wiping her tears away as she managed to control her grief. Geal agreed. There was much to talk about, explain, and figure out. As the family, Geal, and Sneachta went inside, Maelíosa's heart swelled with joy; she had all her sons back once again. It was truly a happy solstice day!

Once inside the brothers told their parents all about their journey and how Micheál had killed Dorcha. This news brightened everyone's day. Ernst was very proud of his sons. Alsandar had made it possible with his magic and Micheál with his courage. If little Torin had not left to return Sneachta home, Dorcha would still be around today. As Maelíosa sat and listened to everyone, she slowly began to realize how big the turn of events really were. So much had changed, and as she listened and watched her sons, she saw how much they had changed. Alsandar and Micheál were now grown men. The journey had welded them into strong, confident people who were capable of so much more than she had ever thought before. Micheál explained how they chose to make the sacrifice in return for the sacrifice Geal Geamhradh had made for the people of the Valley of the Dragon. His parents understood, and though it saddened them, they agreed it was the right thing to do. Geal Geamhradh had done much for them when no one else did. Faeries didn't have to do anything for humans to begin with, and most never did. But Geal had done so and paid a heavy price for it.

Soon the conversation turned to the tower. "Mom, there's another big surprise." Micheál said.

"Did you know we are fearie folk?" Alsandar asked. Maelíosa didn't quite understand. She didn't think Geal would turn them when she had returned her sons to her. She wasn't keeping them, after all.

"What do you mean?" Ernst asked. He had been mostly quiet as he listened to the story of their journey but now felt concerned there was something Geal had not told them. He wondered if she had betrayed them after all.

"We found your grandfather!" Torin said with a big smile on his face.

"My grandfather? What do you mean? Which grandfather?" Maelíosa said.

Maelíosa had never met her mother's father, for he had vanished before her mother was born, and she knew her father's father had passed away already. "What are you talking about, Torin; I don't have any grandfathers anymore," Maelíosa said very confused.

"Well, one of them is alive, and he needs you. He's really sick right now," Torin replied. Geal smiled as she told Maelíosa the real story of her grandparents. Ernst dropped his mug of hot tea from the shock of it. Instead of cleaning it up, he just stared at his wife. He had married a faerie. Well, at least a part-faerie. It now made sense to him though. She was very beautiful and talented. Sometimes he felt she was like magic when it came to her healing abilities, the way she took care of things and her family.

"Will you come to the tower and see Grian Feur, your grandfather?" Geal asked. Geal thought it might solve two problems. Grian would get the care he needed, and maybe, just maybe Ernst and Maelíosa just might like the tower after all.

Maelíosa and Ernst looked at Geal bewildered. "What tower?" Ernst asked.

"Dorcha's tower!" Alsandar replied.

"What!" Maelíosa cried out in shock and disgust.

"It's okay, Mom. Dorcha's tower belongs to Geal now. It isn't Dorcha's anymore," Torin explained. Maelíosa and Ernst were confused. No one had mentioned a tower yet. It was all they could take to listen to their son's story of their journey, being hunted by Dorcha and almost killed by her and the fact the little white dragon was the winter queen's who, by the way, was sitting there having tea with them in their own kitchen! And after all that, they throw in Dorcha's tower. The one place and one person in the whole world they did not want to have anything to do with ever! The past few months had been all she could take to begin with. She wondered where it would all end. Ernst nursed the notion he was still in bed dreaming and that none of this was real. But he knew in his heart it was. Geal saw the confusion and how overwhelming it all was for the two. She wished she could make it all easier on them, but she could not. The facts were what they were. She couldn't change any of it. In time, though, she knew they would come to grips with it all, and things would be well again.

Geal rose from her chair and grabbed the teapot. "Let me get you some more tea," Geal said as she thought of what to say next. She had to get Maelíosa back to the tower as soon as possible to help Grian. Geal filled the teapot with more tea and hot water. She brought it back to the table and sat down once again. Looking at Maelíosa and Ernst, she said, "The tower isn't Dorcha's anymore. It is mine. It is not an evil place now but a happy one. It will be quite safe now to go there. And that is where your grandfather is right now."

Ernst felt uncomfortable going to the realm of a faerie. He wasn't a faerie; he was a man. He had no faerie blood in his veins.

What would happen if he went where no human was allowed? He didn't want to be left behind either. He didn't know what could happen. What if his family never came back? "What about me? I'm human," Ernst asked.

Geal smiled and calmly replied, "Oh, that's okay. You've already been claimed by a faerie." She glanced at Maelíosa with a coy smile and poured her another cup of tea.

Geal didn't want to waste more time explaining things. She wanted to tell them the rest of the story once there. They had left Grian alone far too long as it was. Geal wanted to get Maelíosa there as soon as possible. "We need to go soon. We left him there alone so I could return your sons," Geal explained.

"He's really sick, Mom. He needs you," Torin begged.

Maelíosa took a few seconds to regain her thoughts. Everything had happened so fast, and there had been so much to take in. But finally her instinct as a medicine woman took over. "Sure, sure, let's go. Just give me a minute to put a few things together," Maelíosa said as she rose from her chair. Maelíosa felt butterflies in her stomach at the thought of finally meeting her grandfather, who she had long thought dead and on top of that a Faerie as well. Grabbing her medicine bag, Maelíosa suddenly realized she didn't know what was wrong with him. Turning back to Geal she asked, "What is his malady?"

"Starvation, I think," Geal answered not quite sure how to put into words what Grian's illness really was. He had certainly been starved of light, joy, and love all these years. It was the best answer Geal could think of. They had not yet explained what had happened to him. Geal didn't want to waste anymore time.

"Starvation!" Maelíosa exclaimed surprised. She wondered how faeries could suffer from starvation. They were such powerful creatures. Maelíosa threw what she had to treat such an ailment into her bag. She also wondered how her grandfather ended up in Dorcha's tower.

Chapter 19

E rnst and Maelíosa were flabbergasted by the ride on the wind. It amazed them how fast they traveled over the valley below. Suddenly they were upon the balcony when they had just left the farm only minutes ago. "This way," Geal said as she guided Maelíosa and her family into the tower. Maelíosa and Ernst were held spellbound by the beauty and rich interior of the tower. Their home paled by far compared to the tower. However, as they looked at the bare walls as Geal rushed them down the halls and up stairwells, Maelíosa felt something was missing. Surely with all the rich furnishings, there would be tapestries and such on the walls. Maelíosa wondered why they were so bare as Geal brought them into a warm cozy room. Though the fire had died down to just embers since they left, the stones of the fireplace held the heat quite well. Maelíosa and Ernst were very relieved by the warmth of the room. The ride on the wind had been a little chilly. The sun was now setting, making the light in the room very dim, with only the embers of the fireplace to see by.

While Micheál and Alsandar got the fire going again, Geal lit a candle and handed it to Maelíosa. Maelíosa slowly approached the figure lying in the great ornamental wood-carved bed. She felt a little unsure about how to help the man; she had never treated faerie folk before. Feeling a little nervous, she bent over the figure.

She was startled by his shriveled sunken appearance. He didn't look like a faerie but rather a pitiful creature Maelíosa had no words for. The light of the candle didn't make it much better. It gave the sick faerie a deeply haunted look. Maelíosa reached out to put her hand on his forehead to feel if he had a temperature but then paused. She didn't want to touch the yellowed skin. But as she looked down upon Grian, her heart felt great pity. This was indeed a creature in need and not just any creature but her grandfather. He had to have been through a terrible ordeal to come out looking as pathetic as he did. As Maelíosa gently touched his forehead, Grian's eyes opened to look up at her. A faint smile spread across his lips.

"Aiofa!" Grian whispered, "I have missed you so much, my love." Maelíosa shrunk back. He thought she was her grandmother. Grian reached out to take her hand.

"No, I'm not Aiofa. I am your granddaughter, Maelíosa," Maelíosa said as gently as she could while she held his hand. Grian's eyes grew wide. Suddenly he seemed more coherent as he looked Maelíosa over. A tear rolled down from the corner of his eye as he looked away.

"I'm sorry, you look just like her," Grain replied.

Maelíosa didn't know what to say next. She felt saddened for him. "Is she well?" Grian asked squeezing her hand.

"I'm sorry, Grandfather. She has passed many years now," Maelíosa replied as gently as she could. She didn't want to tell an ailing man bad news. It didn't help them get well when they needed to most. Grian turned his head and cried.

After a few minutes, he stopped and asked, "How long?"

"A long time, ten years now," Maelíosa answered. Grian stared at the ceiling as he thought of his beloved Aiofa. He remembered her smile and charming laugh as they played in the glen together when they fell in love. It wasn't long after that he married her, and then suddenly Grian remembered more. The brothers and

Sneachta drew in closer to be next to the ailing faerie. Torin crawled up to sit next to Grian and took his other hand.

"It's okay, Grandfather, we are here. You have us now," Torin said. Grian turned toward Torin and smiled.

"So my wife and child lived," Grian said.

"Yes, that's Nana, she is still around," Alsandar happily replied. Grian chuckled, "Another Nana."

Geal came to stand next to Maelíosa. Looking down on Grian, she asked, "Grian what happened? You just vanished?"

"I'm curious too," Maelíosa said. "Mom always said you had died in the fire when the cottage burned down. No one even knew how it burned down or what really happened. And then suddenly, here you are."

Grian closed his eyes. He didn't know if he could speak of his ordeal just yet. He felt so weak and heartbroken. Though his ordeal had finally ended, he still felt imprisoned with all his horrid memories of Dorcha and her torments. The long, long years he spent grieving and living in the darkness within and without were still with him. He wasn't sure he would ever be able to get past it all. It was all too fresh in his mind yet. The distant past still seemed like another world to him, or rather a happy dream he had dreamt up before Dorcha took him away from it. Grian closed his eyes and turned his head away. He was tired, so very tired through and through. But then as he felt himself just wanting to go sleep forever, he heard a song. It was a song of the faeries, spoken in their old language. It echoed in his mind and chased away the dark thoughts that still battled for his soul. It was the song he had heard right before he had been rescued. Grian sighed. He felt hope once more.

Seeing that Grian was not up to speaking just yet, Maelíosa turned and mixed a potion for Grian into the snow water Geal had blessed and melted. The snow had been blessed with the light, and together with the herbs, Maelíosa had mixed it all into a warm tea. Lifting Grian's head, Maelíosa helped him drink it all down.

When Grian had drunk all the tea down, he relaxed. For the first time in eighty years, Grian was able to go to sleep. The others watched as he slept.

"Mom say's sleep is good when you're sick," Torin explained to Geal. Geal smiled and ruffled his hair affectionately. It was only a few moments after Grian had fallen asleep that he seemed to morph from a sickly looking creature into a more normal looking faerie. His skin changed to a healthy looking sun-kissed tan and filled out where it had been shallow and sunken. His dried straw-like dirty hair began to shimmer with a golden sheen. Maelíosa was surprised. She was sure it was Gael's snow rather than her herbs that had made such a grand transformation. But Geal assured her it was her herbs as well. Maelíosa was part faerie, after all, so it was as much her magic as it was Geal's. Between the two of them, the potion had worked wonders for Grian. While Grian slept, Geal took Ernst and Maelíosa on a tour of the tower. The brothers stayed behind to watch over Grian.

Room by room and floor by floor, Geal led the two around and told them of all that happened when Geal, Sneachta, and the brothers had cleansed the tower. Maelíosa finally discovered why the tower walls were so bare. Ernst marveled at his sons' courage and at the same time felt horrified at what his sons went through with Geal to clean the tower of Dorcha's dark magic. Ernst felt his heart sink when he learned of the attack on Alsandar by the shadow creatures and grew very angry when he heard of Dorcha's last attempt on the life of his son Micheál. Finally Geal took them down into the dungeon to show them where they had found Grian and told them of how they cleansed the chambers. As they stepped into the first chamber, Maelíosa's eyes grew wide with wonder. All around her was the moonlight she knew now was shining outside. The entire dungeon felt peaceful and calm as if an unseen presence held them warm and sung in its protective arms. "This is incredible!" Maelíosa said.

"Just wait until the sun comes up, it will be like that then," Geal replied.

"This would make a wonderful greenhouse!" Maelíosa said.

"Funny, your sons said the same thing." Geal chuckled. "They're always thinking about you, you know," Geal added. "They want to stay here."

Maelíosa and Ernst didn't reply. Suddenly the wonder and delight of the faerie magic around them dimmed.

Neither of them wanted to leave their sons behind. Though it was a quick trip by the wind, it was a long ways to travel on the ground to come to the tower from their farm. Micheál and Alsandar may have been old enough to stay on their own, but little Torin was not old enough to leave them. "No, I won't lose my son's again," Maelíosa said.

"Neither will I," Ernst said.

"But you don't have too," Geal replied. Geal explained how she needed someone to take care of the tower for her. She had hoped Ernst and Maelíosa might want to live there with their sons. They would have much more land to live on and with the faerie folk so much more to be gained in their lives and especially for Maelíosa's medicinal herbs and plants. Geal explained she would have access to so much more than she had ever had in her life before. "With you here, Grian will surely recover, especially his broken heart. For he will regain his family Dorcha had taken away from him. And when Grian does recover, the Valley of the Dragon will return to its former glory, for it will have the earth faerie return and others like him now that Dorcha is gone," Geal said.

"Earth Faerie?" Ernst asked.

"Yes, Grian Feur is an earth faerie. He makes things grow, and he brings life to barren places. His name means sun grass," Geal explained. "He was named after the great sun faerie, Grian."

"No wonder Maelíosa is so good at growing things," Ernst replied.

As Geal led them to the center chamber, Geal said, "You are of both human and faerie blood, Maelíosa. You can bridge the gap for both sides—you can walk in both worlds. You can live here in ours and still be a part of the world you have always known. Will you think about it?"

"Can my husband come as well? He is not of faerie blood. In fact his family came from a far away land across the sea," Maelíosa said.

"Yes, he's your husband. He can choose," Geal replied.

"Choose? What do you mean 'choose'?" Ernst asked. He wasn't ready to choose to be in one world over the next. The faerie world still confused and frightened him a little, yet he was very curious about the faeries. The idea that he, who was a human, could learn about the faeries on their own soil was very enticing.

"You can choose to stay in our world or the world of humans. It will be okay, just keep choosing every time you want to come and go," Geal laughed.

"Huh?" Ernst sputtered.

"In order to see our world, you choose within to be here; to pass into the human world to be seen by them, you choose within to be there. That is the only way you can go back and forth. That is the way it was with Aiofa once she was sealed to Grian. It is the way for all humans not of faerie blood sealed in marriage to faerie," Geal explained. "However, if you choose permanently, as in commit to only one, you will be in which either choice you made for the rest of your life. So don't ever make up your mind is all you have to do," Geal replied.

"I'll have to think about that. I want both actually. I'm very curious about your world," Ernst said.

"Well, we better get back and check on Grian," Geal said as she turned and led them out of the dungeon.

When Geal, Maelíosa, and Ernst had returned to the room, it was very quiet. Sneachta was coiled in a circle on the hearth rug with little Torin who used his body for a pillow. Both were soundly sleeping. Alsandar had fallen asleep as he leaned over the side of the bed while holding Grian's hand as he sat on a chair. Micheál had fallen asleep in another of the many overstuffed chairs Dorcha had in her tower with a large book slowly slipping off his lap to the floor. Maelíosa hurried over to grab it before it could hit the floor and wake the sleepers. Maelíosa flipped the front open half over to read the cover. It was the book of faerie families. Maelíosa then flipped the book to where Micheál had it left open. There she read Aiofa's and her grandfather's name. It made no mention of her mother's name, Àine. *But then*, thought Maelíosa, *Dorcha would hardly acknowledge such a half-breed that had offended her so since she listed them under Wayward Faeries.*

Ernst looked at the book. It was written in a language he didn't recognize. "You can read this?" Ernst asked his wife. Maelíosa looked at him surprised.

"Of course I can. Why?" asked Maelíosa.

"Because it is all gobbledygook to me," Ernst replied. Geal smiled.

"That is because it is faerie language. Only those of faerie blood can read the writing," Geal explained.

"Do all faeries keep such books?" Maelíosa asked.

"Most do, I think," Geal replied.

Geal never had kept any written record of her family or any faerie family; she had never been married and never had children, so there was never any reason to keep one, no one to hand it down to. No one wanted a freezing wife, and hardly anyone even came to visit her let alone find a romantic interest in her. So Geal never thought about it. She had been around much longer than most faeries, so she knew without having to write about things like which faeries were which and who and where they came from anyway. Being alone most of the time, Geal had a lot of time to think about things. Sometimes her thoughts were her only company except for the snow bunnies and her snow dragons, Bain and Sneachta. The histories of the faeries were ingrained into her memories like words written in stone. But now Geal had a family.

She would always watch over them and be there for them. She wondered how it would be if she ventured out in the spring and summer. She had never done so; until now she never had a reason for it. Would they like to come and visit her? As Geal looked at Ernst and his human frailty, she thought the answer was probably not. He would not last long in her realm unless he were faerie or bound to her. Since everyone was sleeping, Geal, Maelíosa, and Ernst went to sleep as well. It had been a long day for everyone.

Chapter 20

Sneachta opened his eyes first. Forgetting Torin had fallen asleep on him, Sneachta stretched and yawned. Torin rolled off onto the cool floor.

"What the hey!" Torin exclaimed as he suddenly woke up with a thud.

"Oh, sorry!" Sneachta said. Torin sat up and rubbed his eyes. Looking around, he saw everyone else sleeping except his mother. She was nowhere to be seen.

"Where's Mom?" Torin asked.

"I don't know," said Sneachta, "but I smell something good." Torin sniffed but could smell nothing. He wished he could smell like a dragon. Torin watched as Sneachta headed out of the room and decided to follow him. They went down the corridor and two flights of stairs. Torin didn't smell anything yet, but Sneachta sure did. Sneachta hurried faster as he got closer to the source of the smell. After he came to the next flight of stairs, Torin could smell what Sneachta could. He followed quickly after his friend and ran down the steps following a familiar scent that woke him every morning of his life before his journey. The last door at the end of the hall was ajar, and Torin heard his mother humming from within. The smell of her cooking filled the corridor, making Torin's stomach growl and his mouth water. Torin had missed the morning smells of his mother's cooking and hurried even faster as well trying to beat Sneachta to the room. In their haste, Torin and Sneachta both tried to run into the room at the same time. The door banged open as the two fell through landing with a loud thump on the hard stone floor.

"Hey, be careful, you two," Maelíosa chided as she set a large wooden table for breakfast. "Breakfast is almost ready. Go wake your brothers and dad and don't forget Geal," Maelíosa ordered. Torin's stomach growled. He had not eaten in over a day. There had been so much going on he had not even thought about it. But the smells of his mother's cooking made his appetite ferocious.

Torin turned around and flew out the door yelling, "Wake up, everyone, its breakfast!" Maelíosa rolled her eyes.

"I hope he doesn't wake up Grian. He still needs to sleep." Sneachta just shrugged while he politely waited for his breakfast. Maelíosa laughed and placed a large piece of venison in a bowl for Sneachta who quickly gulped it down.

Maelíosa had just finished getting the table ready when the others started to come through the door.

"That smells so good. I'm starving!" Micheál said as he grabbed a piece of bread before he sat down. Maelíosa chided him for not waiting until everyone was seated. "We haven't eaten in days, Mom," Micheál replied as he woofed down the bread.

"Days?" Maelíosa asked, "How is that possible? You don't seem like you're starving."

"It's the Faerie magic," Geal explained as she came into the room and sat down.

"We haven't had time to think about eating," Alsandar added. Just then Torin's father came into the room with Grian leaning on his arm.

"Grian! Are you sure you should be up?" Maelíosa asked surprised. "I'm well enough; your tonic has done miracles for me," Grian replied. Maelíosa watched him as Ernst gently helped Grian into a chair. He looked much better than the last time she had seen him. He was right; he was better. He looked normal, but Maelíosa could tell he was still a little weak. As Grian looked at the food laid out he started to cry.

"I haven't eaten in years," Grian commented as he took in the sight of food and its smell. Little Torin grabbed a plate for him, and Maelíosa loaded it up with bread, oatmeal, and eggs. Geal filled his cup with fresh milk and honey.

Everyone waited until Grian had taken his first bite. He closed his eyes as he savored the taste of food rolling over his tongue. After swallowing, he grinned from ear to ear. "This is indeed the best breakfast I have ever eaten!" Grian said. The brothers and other adults cheered and laughed and then dug in for themselves. It was a happy, noisy breakfast with everyone chattering about how well things had turned out. Geal was very curious about what had happened to Grian, but she had not pressed the issue until she felt sure he was comfortable in his newfound freedom. She knew he would be haunted by his ordeal for many years to come. But she hoped with his family around him, he would do well anyway and get back into life as he used to be.

When breakfast was nearly done, Geal finally had the courage to ask her question again. "What happened to you, Grian? How did you end up here?" Geal asked. The room fell silent as all eyes centered on Grian.

With a full stomach and his family beside him, Grian felt secure and safe. He finally had the courage to face and talk about what had happened to him. The thought of his tormentor being dead gave him peace. Geal and the brothers had told him what had happened to Dorcha when they took him upstairs for the first time since he had been imprisoned. He had been fearful until then that Dorcha would come back and bind him up once more. But Grian knew Dorcha was far away rotting in the earth, never to harm anyone again. As Grian looked at all the faces around the table and his beautiful granddaughter who looked very much like his beloved Aiofa, Grian remembered the day he fell into Dorcha's captivity. Looking down at his hands so he wouldn't have to look at the faces around him, Grian began recanting his epic.

It was the day Aiofa told him she was with child. Dorcha had showed up at their cottage in the woods on the edge of the valley just after Aiofa had left to visit her mother to tell her the good news. He felt sure Dorcha would have killed Aiofa right there and then. Dorcha was furious. Dorcha had threatened to kill Aiofa and the child if Grian did not leave her immediately. Grian was very relieved Aiofa was not there at the time. Dorcha had been infatuated with Grian for many years before he met Aiofa. But Dorcha's obsession had turned into possessive love. Grian was a happy faerie and didn't want to fall in love with a dark faerie, especially Dorcha who was cruel and malevolent by nature. Grian had told Dorcha there could be nothing between them and sent her away from his life. She never bothered him again until that fateful day. Dorcha screamed at him and cursed him for doing the unthinkable, for falling in love with a human. Before Grian could react, Dorcha's jealous fury grew, and before he knew it, she cast a spell to bind him, had Droch torch the cottage, and imprisoned him beneath her tower in darkness and agony. She then tortured and used him and his grief to grow her shadow daemons to weave her dark magic from.

No one said a word after Grian was finished with his story. Maelíosa felt her heart break for both Grian and her grandmother. She remembered her grandmother. She always seemed so sad and quiet all the time. Aiofa had never spoken about what had ailed her, so Maelíosa never knew. Once she had asked where her grandfather was and was told he had taken a very long journey and could never return. As Maelíosa grew up, she finally understood he had died, or so everyone thought. Maelíosa beamed with joy to finally be with her grandfather and stood to give Grian a long warm hug. As she held Grian, they both broke into tears. "What of my child? What is her name? Where is she?" Grian asked as his emotions calmed.

"Mom is fine. She's at home," Maelíosa said.

"Yeah, she's doing good. She's a little weird though but good." Micheál laughed.

"She's weird because she is half faerie. I see that now," Alsandar said. Maelíosa thought about her son's comment.

All these years Maelíosa had wondered about her mother. She was always so different. She never did seem to fit into the rest of the world. Now she finally understood why. "Her name is Àine, and she lives alone in the Glade of the Dragon Egg."

Grian looked up at Maelíosa a little surprised and asked, "She lives alone?"

Maelíosa smiled. "Yes, she prefers it that way, except for Samhain, and then she has all kinds of people around. She throws a great celebration then to honor the dead. People come from around the whole valley!"

Geal suddenly stood up. "Oh my, I've been so silly. I can go get her. She must know her father is alive!" Geal exclaimed as she rushed out of the room.

"So Nana is coming?" Torin asked.

"Looks that way," Maelíosa replied.

"Then we can all live in the tower," Torin said happily. Maelíosa just smiled at her son. She knew her mother would not want to leave her glen and that Grian, once healed, would be gone a lot come spring, healing the Valley of the Dragon. Both she and her husband had not the time yet to discuss where they would stay. The tower was fabulous, especially the dungeon. She already knew in her heart where she wanted to live, but she didn't know what her husband wanted. She would have to wait and see.

It was several hours until Geal returned with Àine. As she was led to meet with her father for the first time, Àine held herself steady and calm. Inside she was very nervous. At first she was very surprised to have the winter queen come visit and even more surprised to learn her father still lived. Àine was also horrified to hear what had happened to her father and sad that her mother never knew. As she walked toward the man in the chair who was supposed to be her father, Àine had many mixed emotions. Grian looked up at her and was very surprised to see a feminine image of himself looking back at him. He had expected her to look like Aiofa. But then he was happy, as he knew Aiofa had always seen a part of him was with her and that he had not left her entirely alone. Àine likewise was surprised to see an image of herself looking back at her. "You look just like me!" Àine and Grian exclaimed at the same time. The two laughed and then hugged.

The sun set and the sun rose twice before the family, Sneachta, and Geal realized so much time had gone by. They were all caught up in talking and sharing their lives with Grian. Time in the faerie realm passed differently than time in the human world. Sleep and hunger often went unheeded without notice when the mind was preoccupied. As each day passed, with the help of Maelíosa's tonics, Grian grew strong and healthy. Finally on the fourth day after the winter solstice, it was time for Maelíosa and Ernst to decide if they would stay in the tower. Geal needed to get back to her icy mountain refuge. She learned she could spend time in the warmth, but the longer she stayed, the less it snowed, and her icy crown began to melt turning to woven stems of flower stalks, and her pale blue skin started to turn into the color of normal flesh.

It was a big decision for Ernst and Maelíosa. They would have to leave their entire lives behind. They felt sad abandoning the only home their family had ever known. But at the same time, they realized that a move to the tower would bring so much more into their lives. It was an uncomfortable choice to make. However, Maelíosa secretly wanted to live in the tower. She just wasn't sure what her husband would want. Maelíosa and Ernst both looked at each other, afraid to choose, not wanting to disappoint the other, while each secretly wanted the same thing. Geal could see their thoughts written on their faces.

With a wily grin, Geal tempted Maelíosa and said, "You would have access to many herbs that are very rare and no human has ever seen before." To entice Ernst, Geal told him how rich and fertile the land around the tower would be because Dorcha had not let her dragon scorch her territory. It was Geal's realm now, and being in the realm of a good faerie meant good land. His struggles would end with the hard land he now had to cope with, and he could provide much for the valley until it returned to its previous health.

"And what about the people of the valley I serve?" Maelíosa asked.

"You can still do what you will as you will. You are of faerie blood, and therefore no faerie law will interfere with your comings and goings," Geal answered. Then with a grin she added, "Unless, of course, you want to expand your practice to the faeries as well." Maelíosa and Ernst agreed to go live with their sons in the tower. It didn't matter where they lived Maelíosa thought. So long as she was with her children. Ernst felt the same way. The family was together again and that which was lost had been found again. The family would be whole once more. Grian was very happy, for he could be with his grandchildren anytime he pleased now. He would stay at the tower during the winter months and then with Àine in the spring and summer and in the fall return to the tower after Samhain.

The brother's journey turned from tragedy to a very happy ending that would last for centuries yet to come. They would be able to stay together as a family with their parents and never have to part again. Ernst would have the best land to grow crops and cattle on, and Maelíosa, having access to many of nature's healing plants, would have the best medical practice for both humans and faeries. Most of all, Torin was happiest about never having to say goodbye to Sneachta. They would be great friends always, and they could see each other all the time. Though Alsandar eventually realized on his own he was never a sorcerer to begin with but a magical creature instead, he felt immense joy knowing he would learn the knowledge of faerie magic, the most powerful magic of all. Micheál was excited about watching Sneachta grow into a powerful great white dragon someday. Turning to the winter queen as she was leaving, Maelíosa asked, "Why have you been so warm and kind to us?"

Geal smiled and looked down at her hands that were comfortably clasped hanging in front of her lap. "Because I am a cold being, and that is the only kind of warmth I am allowed." But most of all, Geal was happy she had new friends and, in her belief, a new family. She had never had anyone except her dragons. Being a cold faerie, she seldom had visitors, and no one really wanted to be around her coldness for long. Her days of being alone were now behind her, and happy days lay ahead for those she helped. Though she felt so very cold on the outside, deep within Geal Geamhradh, the winter snow queen was glowing with warmth.

Epilogue

As one journey ended, another began for the brothers and their parents. The Valley of the Dragon rejoiced in the news that Dorcha would never again haunt their valley, and with the help of Torin Sr., Maelíosa, and Grian, everything would return to normal once again. Micheál eventually became a dragoneer of the faeries, the greatest honor of all, for he would have the best dragons. Alsandar became very gifted in magic since he had access to all faerie magic as well. And little Torin eventually became the king of a new and great powerful magical race born of human and faerie blood that became known as the Eephen. They were the blood of both worlds that became a single new race.